Publication

© Mountains Education Services Trust

reidmess@aol.com

First prepared for publication 2023

Editing: J.A.R.

ISBN:
978-0-6457725-0-0 Hard Copy
978-0-6457725-1-7 e-book

Table of Contents

Part 1 – And so it begins

1. Amy Whitelaw - Cop at the crossroads?

Amy Whitelaw stood on the intersection of George St and Martin Place, in the centre of Sydney, considering her current life and where she might finish up in the next ten years all in the time needed to wait for the pedestrian traffic lights to turn green.

Amy wondered if the intersection she was on was symbolic of the intersection at which her life stood. A university graduate Amy had joined the New South Wales Police Service as a graduate recruit having been recruited into a fast track learning and development program. Promoted to a Senior Constable after two years of service and to Acting Detective sergeant three years further on, during which time she had completed her master's degree in policing.

Amy moved into the Murder Squad almost a year ago. She knew she was a strong applicant to be appointed permanently to the position she currently held on an acting basis. The lights changed and she began to cross.

To have risen to her current acting rank was a sound achievement. Some people she realised had waited most of their working lives to achieve her current level. Some people never did.

It was not that the work was not interesting. She had been involved in catching some well-known criminals, excitement a plenty at times, but there was this nagging suspicion in her mind as to whether she was really a career police person.

Street Cleaner

Any personal relationship that had developed for her, of which there were few, was disrupted and abandoned. Her love of policing was stronger than the desire to develop any lasting relationship no matter how handsome or charismatic was the man involved. She was always pretty much on call and if not on call the job preoccupied her mind.

The job had conspired against her having a normal life. Boyfriends, who were not put off by her being called out, were put off by her lack of attention, when they were together. Some men seemed to understand her situation but did not want a sometime relationship.

Amy also neglected long time female friends. No time for catching up for coffee, shopping, or even and especially a much-needed weekend away. She missed the intimacy of chatting with a trusted friend.

Some of her graduate friends were earning far more than her, though their employment was less secure. Financial security what person needs it in their twenties or even in their early thirties? Let's have some cash, and some time to spend it. Oh, I wish she thought.

Amy thought to herself that she would wait and see whether she succeeded in gaining the Sargent's position permanently. Maybe putting off a solution would allow life to sort itself out. Amy thought of a quote from one of her classes on management and leadership:

"No decision is a decision. You are accepting the status quo, which, may be catastrophic or just perfect"

Street Cleaner

As she walked towards work, she pushed back her blond hair and reciprocated a smile from a passing attractive male. She made her way up Martin Place passed the grand, old bank buildings, which were now expensive hotels and boutiques. Banking no longer needed buildings. Cafes and government offices including the Sydney office for the Prime Minister were coming into Amy's view.

She passed the studio of a leading television station on her way up the plaza. Amy had slowed her stride for a quick look in the window. "Isn't he" she said to herself, then paused in her unfinished observation and completed it by speaking to herself in hushed tones, "what does it matter, it is just trivia, the job calls its wife," and continued on in a self-imposed silence towards work.

****

Street Cleaner

Amy may have in her mind stood at the crossroads of her life but she was unaware of events that were occurring over the "ditch" in Auckland, New Zealand and how it would affect her in the coming years. Less than two years on from this conversation with herself she would be leading an investigation to find and stop a deadly killer.

A Street Cleaner not of the mechanical kind was about to start cleaning the streets. Ridding them of what the cleaner considered to be human pariahs who were not generally punished for their misdeeds and even if they were caught managed the system to suit their own ends

2. A street Cleaner begins to take shape

While Amy was walking in Sydney, the man nick named "Jug", because his mates always thought he was the full bottle, was on holiday in New Zealand. Well maybe not really a holiday. It was certainly not the holiday that he had originally intended. It was to be a time away to defuse, to put aside the anguish he felt about the lack of real punishment for crimes committed in his homeland, Australia. The time away to holiday had now been transformed into a time to see justice done, a time to kill, to deep clean the unpunished to create clean safe streets.

As in his home country, he knew that wherever he went there would still be perpetrators of crimes that went unpunished or lightly punished, a rap on the knuckles, not even that sometimes. Like Australia his holiday destination had its share of the unpunished. He wanted to see if he was up to eliminating those people, he found unacceptable members of society.

****

Standing in the shadows, with the on again, off again rain beating on his face, he contemplated his first victim. Was this his first and last or the first one of many? Could the kill satisfy his lust for justice or would it be never satisfied?

What would it feel like for him to impose the justice he required to be metered out by society that was not delivered through the system, on his chosen victim? Would he feel vindicated? Would he feel righteous? Would he be repulsed with himself? Different thoughts were running through his mind, but not so many as to distract him from the task at hand. There was much to occupy the mind as the soon to be killer waited.

As he walked almost silently behind but just out of sight of his intended victim his mind turned to the justice he sought. The plea bargains, the so called information on others given to the police to mitigate their own punishment was a way to circumnavigate justice. The influence pedalled by some criminals in helping people to secure power, whether it be political, monetary or for passion, would be repaid to the crim if and/or when they were eventually caught. Not bribes. No, no just a favour repaid.

The placement of associates of a particular criminal in places of influence mainly within governments and also in various private enterprises, particularly where capital is needed and accepted, without too many questions being asked would secure a willing or even an unwilling allegiance that would be called upon at some future time.

Help provided to smart lawyers early in their career may at some time in the future result in niches in the law being found that may allow evidence to be supressed or help for parliamentary members to be elected who could have legislation repressed or even help given to an ordinary person who needed a hand from their "local crim" today could yield a lifetime fealty and usefulness to a "crim".

Back to the task at hand, eh was approaching the soon to be victim. He could not believe this man, Gabriel Asiago, now only a short distance away, a known crime lord in New Zealand who had escaped justice through plea bargaining and informing on one of his criminal competitors was walking alone. Where was his protection, why had they let him go out without at least one of his 'associates'? An old song began in the brain of the soon to be killer, which intoned the notion that you "only live twice". Why that song he thought?

It was 2:30 in the morning, so maybe this unpunished felon, as the soon to be murderer thought of his intended victim, had left home of his own accord. Seemingly unknown to anyone the future victim trod the darkened streets unaware of the fate that was about to befall him. Was he stealing a moment away from his always present protection guard? Was the intended victim one of those who now relished the time they had been gifted?

The soon to be punished appeared to be relaxed and carefree in his taking of this night time sojourn.

The intermittent rain of the last few hours continued. As both men walked, they would soon be in each other's way. Till the attack occurred only one knew such a meet up was not accidental.

The killer was tracking his victim on foot. It was time to go closer to the future victim to come closer to delivering the killer's version of justice. "Jug" our killer, moved silently across several yards, following a path he had mapped out so as not to be seen and unlikely to be heard. He closed in on his prey shielded by the lack of streetlight. Camouflaged in black clothing, including gloves with a blackened area under his eyes he blended into the dark of the night with the moon obscured by scudding rain. Seconds to go, a second to go and the victim was there.

As the victim passed the location of the soon to be murderer, the killer lunged from the shadows stabbing the unsuspecting victim in the back. He expected the man to fall. His vengeance to be swift and complete but the stabbed man did not go down. Not a deadly blow.

Was he inept in his now chosen hobby the killer asked himself, without speaking? Why didn't he go down? The victim wounded but still mobile began to turn while searching in the right pocket of his coat.

As the victim turned, "Jug" lunged forward and stabbed the knife into the chest of the victim, where he believed the heart to be. Then the knife struck the target yet again, and the victim began to fall. A tremendous feeling of relief suddenly came upon the killer. Surprisingly the victim did not call for help with only a strangled cry to be heard. He stabbed the victim again several more times just to be sure the task had been completed. No discernible signs of life. It was over.

The people who lived on this street, the killer believed would no doubt applaud him now they were rid of this societal problem. For a moment the killer, thought of himself as a superhero. A life gone, a problem solved.

This fleeting thought was replaced with the reality of leaving the scene without leaving evidence of his crime. He muddied the scene. The rain would wipe out all evidence. With the victim now dead there would be no more loss of blood.

He quickly searched his fallen victim. In his right-hand coat pocket the killer discovered a 9mm pistol. A short silencer was fitted to the weapon, but it was still possible the gun could be carried concealed in the victim's large coat pocket. "Jug" had another weapon for next time, if there was to be a next time. Would there be a next time? The thought briefly flashed across his mind?

It was beyond time to go. Adrenaline had flooded his body. He was now feeling dizzy with relief or was it fear? He checked around once more for any evidence of his presence at the murder scene. The stark light emitting from his phone showed a half shoe print in the grass adjacent to the cement path which was quickly erased by water scooped from a gutter.

The street was clothed in darkness, apart from a streetlight much further along the street He judged it to be too far from his position for anyone who wandered by to make a positive identification of him or of his victim from afar. As he left the murder scene confident that no one had seen him, he examined the gun. It looked relatively easy to use. He had used guns during his army life straight out of school.

Now a few minutes after the attack he was not as happy with the outcome as he thought he would be, he walked away still questioning himself but not speaking. Is this what he really wanted, to be a killer? No matter how he rationalised his service to the community and righting of his perceived wrongs by the justice system, he was suddenly afraid. Afraid of what might happen to him if he were caught, afraid of what he had become and then he was afraid of himself.

There was also regret and sadness. As a murderer he felt many things, but he truly did not know what he really felt.

Several minutes had gone by since the death of his victim. The rain was heavier and had washed away most of his victim's blood that had sprayed onto his black jacket. The rest he wiped off as he walked with a black rag he had brought with him.

****

He had now long left the scene and was travelling by foot back to his hotel. Greeted by the front of house manager, "It's wet tonight." An obvious statement meant as a greeting not as a weather report. "Indeed, it is", replied the newly minted killer, crouching a little so as to ensure his full profile could not be seen in case any spatter of blood he had not removed drew attention.

Time continued apace. It seemed so long ago the killer had delivered his version of justice, but it was only an hour. As he entered his room a mixture of emotions were still swirling through his head which were evidenced on his body through short periods of physical pain and occasional violent shaking. Suddenly grief, then satisfaction, remorse surely not, anger. Was the job really done or was this just the start?

A fitful sleep, interrupted by vision of the murder but each time in a new location, the first time in a public square somewhere, but not in the country where he could be currently found. Cheering of a crowd who almost filled the square accompanied his actions in killing his victim but with a silent glum, serious looking group of men and women dressed in dark suits standing in the far-left hand corner of the plaza beckoning him to come to them. In this dream he started to move towards them. The closer he got the better he heard a chant:

"You are one of us. You are one of us." "

Jug" in his sleep approached a man who looked like his victim, who as he got close began laughing mockingly:

"You didn't get me. You didn't get me".

He always awoke before he reached the man. The dream repeated several times but in different locations, each time concluding with being jolted awake bathed in sweat.

It was early. Breakfast time heralded a new day. His mind leaping between sadness and joy he tried and eventually achieved the feat of eating a filling breakfast in the dining room. Not a total success, more left on his buffet plate than he had eaten, but enough to fill his requirement for renewing of his strength at least to what he regarded as a survivable level. He had adopted a hint from a person that often travelled to jobs at night:

"If you can't sleep, fuel up on solid food to get you through the day".

A premise he believed to be true, based on his own past experiences.

Retiring to his room sometime after breakfast, he played with his new toy. He ejected ammunition from the gun which

he reloaded with a self-satisfying level of speed and accuracy.
More sleep was needed. He took a sleeping pill lay on top of
the now made bed and slept through most of the day.
Waking at around four the same day with a headache that he
knew was brought on by the sleeping tablet, he read for a
while in between disturbing thoughts entering his mind.

He considered his decision to take a next step, another kill,
another clean up or should he stop. He had one more job
that could be done and only a few days left in this 'holiday' to
complete it. But should he stop at one death or clean up a
slew of high-profile escapees from justice.

Yes, but not today. Maybe it could be tomorrow or some
other day, but not today. There would be an extension of his
holiday and another kill before he returned to Australia.

After the second kill, he went straight to the airport waiting
lounge, and checked in. It would then be over for him.
Someone else could continue the quest. He was out. This
would be enough for him. Farewell to the land of the long
white cloud and home to the great southern land, Australia.
He thought it was over for him. But inside two years he
would resume his killing spree but back in his home land of
Australia.

Street Cleaner

Part 2 - Murder in Sydney – does anyone care?

3. Amy Whitelaw – Crime fighter

Arriving for a new shift, it seemed to Amy Whitelaw she had only just left. It had just gone 5:45 AM, awakened by a barking dog on the street after finishing up on a case which looked like an accident to her rather than a murder. A car had reversed down a driveway killing an unsuspecting ordinary husband and father driven by his wife who had gone into shock. The wife was screaming at the scene but had gone into a cationic trance by the time she got to the hospital. Amy had finished the preliminary investigation after mid night.

Amy was tired. She had not slept well. An early night was needed. Less work related night time activity and more time refreshing the body was required. She turned over and tried to go back to sleep. The phone rang.

'Hi Amy', came the happy phone call from 'Bible.' Always a bright voice in the sea of often lack lustre humanity. Bible was seemingly without ceasing always dispensing happiness here and there. He was almost always bright and given to somewhat to misusing quotes from the Bible to encourage everyone around him.

"Evidence is gathered before the sun rises", Bible went on. 'Hardly likely' replied Amy wondering how Bible could always be bright, regardless of the time of day. A murder needed to be investigated.

She rose and looked at herself in the dressing table mirror. Why don't the felons kill in the daytime? Why is so much of the work of criminals carried out in the dark?

Amy was now an Acting Inspector, university educated with a Master's degree. She enjoyed support from her superiors, through the family name. Her father had been a police officer, who retired as a much admired Inspector. The family name made her well regarded, and noticed.

However, she was making her own statement, regardless of name. Results were up since she had been in the Acting role of Inspector. For some of her superiors the results she achieved were not admired. Too much too fast made them feel uncomfortable.

Amy though could readily point to past promotions based on merit rather than any personal relationship to a former officer. Still some of her "supporters" in the police hierarchy gave support unwillingly. It was not that they did not believe she was a good cop. Their problem was that she was a good cop.

Amy knew that some of the members above her feared over time that she might get into a position of leadership backed by the legitimate power of a higher position. Once she got into a position where she could influence those that mattered in the force, changes could occur for the paper shufflers. The reluctant supporters may be pushed back into active policing or into retirement. A happy non-involved life, but doing important work they said, important police roles. Amy had made it clear without offending anyone that real policing was on the streets, in the community where the felons lived and worked along-side their victims.

Strategic plans those above said they were working on. Such time serving activity for those in the police hierarchy sounded good but meant little if there were more felons on the street. Change could lead to new priorities, new skills and new levels of fitness required. She was smart, the smart enemy of those currently directly under the commissioner who were waiting peacefully for their retirement. She knew she was their enemy.

Amy had thought yet again as she showered and dressed of whether the force was what she really wanted for her life. These were much the same thoughts she had had, when becoming a Sergeant. Now she was up for Inspector

The endless long hours of unpaid overtime in times of cold and heat as the year cycled through its seasons. The endless hours she would out in waiting for something, anything to happen.

The never ending paperwork cascading in by computer with files and paper files finding themselves a new home as they feel from her desk onto the floor. More of it once is she became an inspector. Not difficult but do we need so much?

What of that other life? Being an acting inspector gave her even less time than being a sergeant. Someone special, together travelling the world, settling back sometime in the future into the glorious surrounds she now lived but did not often see in the northern beaches of Sydney, maybe some children, though her maternal urge was not strong. The travel would ensure she appreciated where she now lived.

Amy was now in her early thirties, thirty two to be precise. Not old but not so young. She pulled herself up. Such thinking was pointless as no one gets younger.

Medical research had allowed women to give birth into their forties and sometimes even into their fifties. Developments in exercise science and physiology had enhanced the health of people as they got older. If she wanted a child, she thought then there was still plenty of time

Her mind drifted back to sleep. Eight hours sleep, certainty no less than seven was a long-held principal she believed was necessary for keeping the body functioning at an optimal level and the brain working as a thinking, reasoning unit. Such an approach to sleep was supported by academics that appeared in the media who were in turn supported by eminently respectable exercise experts.

Six hours, not even seven was for today. Amy had things to do. Who could afford to let the whole night be lost in sleep? There are bodies to see, witnesses to be questioned and post-mortems to witness.

Now in her car looking for a parking spot she thought of the monotony of a job, which she had loved for so long, was taking its toll. It had started with excitement, the anticipation of being part of an investigative team that at some time in the not too distant past had peaked and been replaced by the hum drum of often doing back up work and desk bound research. For some people it represented a great life. She had thought often of those police shows where the person at the home base was able to sift through information to provide a break through or at least the basis for a further line of investigation that almost always led to a successful outcome.

The Bridge a series was set in two European countries. The common element in each murder being that the victim was found on or near a bridge. Amy had watched the series over its four distinct seasons with a new case each season featuring actors who played the role of police with lives distinctly different from hers. There never seemed to have any paperwork to do. Erratic behaviour was part of the character of the series lead, "Saga Norén". The ability of "Norén" to ignore social norms and behave such that she may have an undiagnosed Asperger's syndrome, among other mental illnesses evidenced by the character's inability to be involved in everyday social interaction as well as exhibiting a lack of empathy. Amy always wondered how the lead was so successful yet so distant from everyone even for much of the time from her police partner.

Norén and her partner(s) seemed to be backed up by a research detective back in the office who was thorough and ingenious at locating people and analysing data. Amy believed that this character was one with a superior insight into human character, possibly a life form from another planet inhabiting the body of an earthling and if not the character was certainly a figment of someone's vivid imagination with no reference in fact.

Now at the location of her office she continued he thoughts about Norén. However, the character of Norén was a committed police officer, continually thinking about her work oblivious to her blunt approach to others. Norén was committed to her job. The only people she seems to care about at all were on rare occasions her police partners, though her approach to them was fraught with concern. She did not seem to have much time to care about herself. But Saga Norén got results. Her behaviour though alarming to her superiors is outweighed by her capacity to get results. "I get results and also fit into the culture", Amy muttered to herself.

"I am no Saga Norén", said Amy to no-one but herself. "Why can't I be allowed to get results without all the paperwork? Let me out. I am ready for some action." Amy now in the office was now screaming and when she was approaching her desk did she realise it. Fortunately, no one noticed apart from two detectives who were too far away to make sense of what she was saying. "Just rehearsing for an interview with a suspect" she called. They looked away.

Her life was more about just sitting and watching, analysing, reading for long periods of time. This was not a way to spend time that would drive Amy to any great heights of intellect or enhance her satisfaction with her work. Seemingly she was pidgin holed, as an academic cop, not a true detective.

Arriving at her desk, the officer's room which she entered looked as cluttered as usual, with the same tired people. Yet another shift with the same old faces the same complaints and the same urgency in their tired movements. Commitment but a lack of energy amplified by restricted resources and by the priorities that for many of them seemed to detract for the reason they believed that police existed.

The job, any job, she had aspired to now was a burden, a necessary requirement to pay the rent.

When would she be at the heart of an investigation? Not just someone that tagged along and did the leg work. Someone had tagged her as the "Backup Queen".

After some years as a detective, having been in financial crimes before joining the murder squad is was time for her own case. "It is time to lead not just the support" she muttered to herself.

Something she wanted to change was the poor work of others. The half-done interviews, the incomplete searches and the let's get it over with approach to policing. She was thorough, so Amy was asked by the boss to pick up on those details that others missed.

Her strength had become a burden with Amy doing nothing but reviewing the work of others. She knew it was time for her to take charge. Let's get it right. She stopped herself from screaming with those around her hearing a muffle cry which some thought was a recaptured sneeze.

Ten years in all in the job, university trained having completed her master's degree she thought she was equal to others around her though she still had the status of one of the junior officers as a Sergeant or even as an acting inspector. It wasn't that she was a woman it was just that she had to take her turn, to pay her dues.

'Whitelaw', the Detective Superintendent yelled to her. "Briefing in ten minutes. We had a murder overnight. James

Street Cleaner

Harrison (recently released from prison) was shot last night. You're heading up the case, at least till some of the senior staff get back on the job. For the time being you are on the front-line Acting Detective Inspector"

At last, Amy could show she was more than the "Back up Queen" Knowing the history of the victim, she wondered, "Harrison murdered. Does anyone care?"

4. The Cleaner – back home.

While Amy Whitelaw was about to start on the new case, the "Street Cleaner" was pondering what had reactivated his wish to kill. He had suppressed the urge since the two New Zealand kills. Almost two years without a kill. He thought he had put it all to bed. The counselling and medication had helped but the continued inability of the justice system to apply appropriate penalties for crimes committed had eaten away at him during the almost two years, since his return to Australia from New Zealand. Ultimately nothing had dimmed his need to see real penalties imposed on the guilty. He believed each day that he should metre out real justice he had now killed twice on his return to Australia.

In his flat, back home, the train rumbled aside the building creating a spa affect, a whirlpool in the bath, where the Cleaner was sitting. The effect was pleasant on the body which half sat and half lay in a soft light from an adjoining room.

The blood that had splashed on the killer's clothes and on his skin had left the body and from the clothes upon which he sat in his bath and swirled about to the edges of the bath collecting and disappearing into the water. The water mixed with the blood provided a short transformation to a red colour followed by a light shade of pink. Both colours were to his liking. The few remaining spots of blood gathering at the opposite the end of the bath soon diluted such that their appearance had never occurred.

The pleasant water was a contrast to the sweat of the night that came from the tension of the wait, not the exertion of the kill. The waiting was the worst. Though the information he gathered on the target as to which was the best location to eliminate the man was correct, the waiting had been long, often filled with painful thoughts. Now anticipation, concern over his detection and arrest monopolised his post kill thinking.

The street had been cleaned. Well at least the cleaning had begun. Another injustice now remedied. The body of the Cleaner now needed to be refreshed for a new day ahead. He had thought he was out. But It was too much for him to see justice flaunted. He knew it was his time to step up.

A thought came to the Cleaner which was verbalised to an audience of one, "they have only just begun to die"

5. James Harrison – Dead at Market and York

Amy knew of James Harrison. Harrison was a man that had come from a privileged background. At one time upon his release from prison he said to the media he had chosen to live on the other side of the law. He had not enjoyed school, but still did better than many others in getting into university with little effort. Having successfully completed his studies he dropped out of sight working in the shadows.

Life on the other side, the dark side of life had started in early in high school for James Harrison where he ran book making facilities for fellow privileged school friends. He facilitated his friends betting on future events, how many suspensions at his school would be handed out in a term as well as more conventional gambling pursuits such horse racing, basketball games and other exotic bets. It had been suggested by old classmates that sometimes James had predetermined the outcomes of school based activities allowing him to accurately frame a market. Though there were always accusations, there was little tangible proof of these childhood accusations.

He used an old-fashioned cockatoo on the lookout when school activities were going on. Pay offs and forgiveness of debts generally kept James Harrison out of trouble. Only a few misdemeanours were ever proved in his adolescent years. The school handing out short term suspensions, which in turn gave him more time to frame markets for those who wished to bet. Short term punishment ensured that school-based misdemeanours stayed in house and news of them never went further into the outside world. The local police suspected that the school organised its own version of "plea deals", with the odd police investigation of a complaint by a member of the public never going anywhere.

Amy had wondered why Harrison had not spent his time in the drug trade. Drugs such as Ice, the curse of which gripped so many of the young bodies and minds, which offered temporary fortunes for many of the current criminal breed turned out not to be one of Harrison's passions. In the one interview Amy Whitelaw had conducted with Harrison he had said he was old fashioned. He liked approaches such as the fix that came with past posting in horse racing the practice of allowing people to bet on a race when you knew the outcome, not the fix of drugs which led to brain drain even though some users had temporary lift into false, temporary creativity. He wanted to take people's money not their lives.

Harrison had several years back spoken on one of those magazine shows on televisions. 'If they are dead then I can't collect from them. Drugs may provide a short term release from the pressures and boredom of life but long term they dry up your soul, short circuit your brain and if they don't kill you leave you as a shell of your former self. I can't work with or collect from a dead brain'

At university where he majored in politics and media, Harrison had spent his time offering fellow students short term loans. He was not a pay day lender but rather a graduation day lender. Borrowers were counting on big jobs and big dollars to repay their loans that would come after they had served their time, completed their penance required, for completing their degrees. Harrison offered money now, to feel what was like when you got there and got that job.

Universities were filled with people that wanted the same things that everyone wanted. Who was going to wait for three or four years or even two and half with a fast-track program for the good things of life? Why wait, advertised Harrison, I can help you out now.

Students sought out Harrison or more correctly his various agents, touts, who looked for people who wanted to live a big life. Harrison's agent, touts, did not approach just students but also tutors, lecturers and researchers as well as admin staff. Most everyone on campus had heard of Harrison's loans. The interest rates were almost as competitive as some commercial loans. Not the same scrutiny required by a bank for taking out a loan.

Short term loans were the most expensive with an asking price of $12 repayment for each $10 borrowed on a six-month loan. No security, little paperwork apart from access to your bank accounts in case you could not repay the loan on time. If that did not work no one was told what would happen but rumours suggested the consequences may be a health rather than a wealth hazard.

Harrison had no shortage of touts wanting to work for him so they might supplement their meagre unskilled working or non-working existence. There were also attempts at competition. He seemed to have the contacts to know when to move out of the way and shut down or move temporarily his central operations from one campus to another campus and stay out of the grasp of his avid competitors. He was legal as he had a money lenders license. Most of his potential competitors were not legal.

When news of his death broke, much of his supposed past in crime as an adolescent was revealed by the electronic media as was his arrest and then release on charges of extortion and murder. A wealthy friend, Alex Chan with whom he had business dealings in Asia had an untimely departure from this earth. Harrison was the prime suspect. They had, had a partnership conducting business activities together. Money was supposed to be missing from their business account. Several witnesses had seen them arguing but Harrison's girlfriend had witnessed Chan having words with another of Chan's business partners about his need for cash and suspicion shifted though nothing was proved.

The Chan case against Harrison had folded. A small-time crook named James Clementi was arrested on a break and enter charge and confessed to the killing of Chan. Harrison was cleared. Clementi had said that he tried to rob Chan in the street. Chan fell and hit his head. The attempted robbery had all gone wrong. It was an accident. Clementi had pleaded guilty to attempted robbery occasioning death.

However, medical evidence did not back the story of a fall without being pushed. The sentence was six years non-parole for Clementi. It was said he took a fall for someone else as his family moved from the western suburbs of Sydney to the Northern Beaches not long after his conviction.

Harrison continued his free and easy life. Now he was dead.

Street Cleaner

"Whitelaw, are you coming?" The bark of the Superintendent woke up a sleeping, standing Amy Whitelaw, who came alive from her self-centred thoughts and began hurrying to the briefing room.

6. The witnesses – "A weird mob"

The briefing was led by Superintendent John Chapman. A man in his mid-fifties a lifelong member of the force. He never had another job as he joined from school at 18. Everything he knew about policing, he learned inside the force mostly on the job.

John Chapman did not get to where he was by following a university pathway. Not a strong believer of external learning. He had been heard saying that "learning about policing outside the force is just pollution of the mind"

He started doing traffic duty and worked his way through a variety of jobs, taking up offers of secondments and being prepared to take policing jobs many would not want. He spent four years in vice. The word was that this was an area of policing he suffered through rather than enjoyed. When he got to the level of Inspector in the major crime area it was where he felt he belonged. Those that knew John well suggested he was happier in this area than he had been for years. He had reached a level working in an area of police work that suited him. Some of his colleagues, peers and subordinates believed he had found his true home and that the journey upward would stop here.

He started the briefing, 'the shooting had occurred last just after 5:15 AM. The on-scene police, responded to two 000 calls, found some people had heard shouting on Market Street close to the corner of York but there is one witness that has been found that claims to have seen the shooting,' He outlined what they had so far found out.

"Another witness heard arguing between what they thought were two men and then two shots but had not seen the people who were arguing nor saw any of the shooting. The witness looked out her window in a consulate where she was working, not long after the shots were fired and had said she had seen a large man, as far as she could tell, walking away from the murder scene. He was heading onto George Street where he turned right heading in in the direction of the town hall. A large man dressed in a long black coat was the extent of the description taken by the attending officers.

Two other witnesses stated they heard two shots and looked out of an office window where they had been pulling an all-nighter to complete a bid for a tender, though they had taken a break for a quick "power nap", these witnesses said they were awake at the time of the shooting. They saw a man face up on the ground. Someone was standing over him. The shooter may have touched the body. The man standing fired at the man on the ground. The suspect could have been a man, but they did not see any facial features. Again, their only description of the shooter was that it was someone in a black coat. The perpetrator walked from the scene and disappeared down the street towards George. They did not see which way the suspect turned when he got to George Street.

We do have one witness an apparently homeless man, though I am told his clothes were kempt. He was sleeping nearby. He stated to the attending police he saw two people arguing then a man appeared out of the dark, spoke to, and then shot Harrison, while the other man ran away. He has not been interviewed in full. He was ill, ill not drunk, at the scene and was taken by ambulance to St. Vincent's Hospital.

Once the identity of the deceased was established, more local police attended and took preliminary statements. These have been typed up and available on your way out.

Local police visited Harrison's home and spoke to his girlfriend. She was unsure who he was meeting other than she understood that he had a meeting with a business colleague. Of course, she was distressed.

With no other information to hand the briefing turned to a preliminary examination of the body confirmed that two shots had hit the victim. The autopsy still needed to be completed but there was no evidence at this stage of anything left by the shooter including the shell casings that appear to have been taken from the scene.

'That is about all we know so far, any questions?' finished Chapman though his packing up of his notes into a file with no eye contact with the group. He was more a let's get on with it person than someone who wanted to analyse the paucity of information usually available at the start of a case,

"All right it is now 6:45 and the local police have handed the case to us. They have as usual cordoned off the scene. Acting Inspector Whitelaw you are to coordinate this investigation at least for the early stages with Menzies as your sergeant. Other officers will be added to your squad today or at the latest tomorrow. Interview the witnesses we know about and see if there are other witnesses in the area. I want door to door in the area, get uniforms onto it", directed Chapman.

"There are currently three uniforms immediately available for door to door and two Detectives will be assigned to you'.

Amy was surprised. Some of the tiredness was gone, replaced with anticipation of the day ahead. She at least had temporary charge with her new partner Kalum Menzies. She had been allocated a group of people to assist, some of whom were probably raw, new appointees without a lot of experience but still she had some resources she would need to manage.

"Yes boss' she almost yelled with renewed vigour

Amy could feel her brain starting to tick over. Responsibility, resources and control, Amy was in charge. At least at the moment she was not the back-up queen. The case was now looking like the active policing for which she aspired.

Amy was now in charge of the Harrison case. Was she ready? Now that she had charge of a case doubts appeared in her mind where only a few minutes ago there had been dissatisfaction with her lot in life. Could she lead a team?

The superintendent finished with words, 'the rest of you, keep working on the "Sparrow" Green case."

"Sparrow" Green whose real name was Bilal Green had been stabbed. The son of a Lebanese Mother and Australian father he was a well-known stand over man. Green was an enforcer who had been charged and been convicted of various types of violence and fighting when his victims decided to fight back. His main role was that of a debt collector. He would remind people of the money they owed usually borrowed from the criminal fraternity. Not financing by Harrison

This was financing that would not be available from the usual financial sources, though the legitimacy of all financiers including licensed banks had come under scrutiny in 2018 Royal commission when they were exposed for unethical if not illegal practices such as charging dead people fees, insurance to cover credit card debt which was worthless as well as charging people for services not provided.

There was an urban myth that Sparrow had approached some of the large banks to help them with debt recovery, given his expertise with recovery of loans from "non-standard" financial; sources. It was no more than a myth though, probably put about by Sparrow.

He also had a side business in providing equipment for criminal enterprises - tools for burglary, a press for printing phony money and generally anything that would be needed for committing a crime. As he was collecting for the financiers, he often also collected for himself.

There was no evidence at the scene of Sparrow's murder to indicate who might be the killer. No witnesses. No one heard anything. The beauty of the knife, little noise except for the noise of victim, expelling their last words, the oxygen in their lungs or a scream, though in Sparrow's case he probably would not have made any noise to not give, his killer any satisfaction, even in death.

Sparrow had been stabbed several times by someone who knew where to do the most damage. It was clear that the assailant had been close to Sparrow when the stabbing occurred, which lead the investigating group to believe that he knew his killer. Though, plenty of people did not like Sparrow, the list did not provide any leads. The usual reliable informants had not come up with anything so far. There had been no recent threats that his family and business associates knew of. No one unusual came to his funeral. His death passed out of the consciousness of the media and the public as the usual dramas of national and international politics and continuing deaths in small wars around the world along with speculation as to whether promised tax cuts made some years earlier would come into effect replaced the death of one Sparrow Green as a headline. A small-time criminal had passed into history, with some people relieved but most people indifferent.

The investigation had not turned up much. The body had been found by an early morning jogger at around 5:30 in the morning. Still dark this time of year, the jogger had said that he had almost tripped over the body. Forensic investigation showed that the scene had been cleaned. The forensic team had found nothing at the scene that indicated who the killer was except that it was evident that the scene had been cleaned. No rubbish, no fibres, no murder weapon which almost certainly had been a short knife almost always used for skinning small game such as rabbits. There was only Sparrow's body and his blood spread on the ground around him as if he had been laid on a carpet of red. Nothing from the post mortem apart from that he was in reasonable health for a man of his age and that the cause of death was due to loss of blood as a result of the stabbing.

Street Cleaner

Nothing of the Sparrow Green case remained in the immediate thinking of Amy who had a new case. My case, not a tag along as she felt she and Kalum had been on the Sparrow Green case. The Green case had so far gone nowhere. "Pursuing multiple lines of enquiry", so the media comment goes. It was time for Amy and Menzies to begin their pursuit of the Harrison case.

7. Kalum Menzies – The Sergeant, Aerial Elmira, and who is Johnathan Lewis-Brown?

Amy and her partner, Acting Detective Sergeant Kalum Menzies, a mixture of English stock and third generation Australian, gathered their temporary crew of uniforms and stood at the murder scene at 7:15 AM. Listening to information gathered by the local police. Together they also surveyed electronic maps of the area around the murder scene to check on any places of past interest in other cases, which may relevant to their investigations.

Kalum came from the western suburbs of the city. He liked where he lived in a small but comfortable house at Penrith in the far west of greater Sydney about 70 kilometres from the city. The location was in Thornton a large newish subdivision adjacent to the rail station and shops built on land previously owned by Defence. The small suburb was a mixture of medium height apartment buildings as well as detached cottages. Thornton was one of many new estates springing up in the west. Unlike other estates, shops, schools, and transport was close by.

Kalum was currently an Acting Sergeant. Amy knew that Kalum wanted to make the "acting" permanent but not in homicide. He wanted to be close to home somewhere west of the city preferably west of Parramatta if possible.

The Acting Sergeant lived in one of the detached cottages which stood on small blocks of land at the back of the Thornton estate as far away as was possible from train noise. He like his wife Judy was a native of the area. Judy was a primary school teacher who worked within the area and was happy with the life in her domain. They both possibly saw themselves moving maybe a few kilometres west to the Blue Mountains a series of mountains, (though some critics suggested they were little more than hills), and pleasant small villages to west of the boundaries of greater Sydney.

Both were happy with their life together. No children yet but only married a few years. Kalum's parents had moved east to take in the distant views of the city of Sydney and had bought a top floor apartment in Parramatta, twenty-five kilometres from the centre of Sydney. Kalum had told Amy he had no desire to follow them though Parramatta was still in the west.

His current job offered more money and enhanced his position for future promotion, but Kalum would be glad to be back working in the west. He felt the centre of Sydney harboured a disingenuous citizenry and people were more genuine in the west.

The shooting had occurred not far from the junction of Market and York Street one being, a so-called homeless man, so the Superintendent had surmised who had been admitted to hospital overnight. He would be first port of call for Amy and Kalum. The rest of the team needed to get on the street. Amy briefed the uniforms about what to ask and look for. Any unusual behaviour seen by near-by residents should be recorded.

Housing predominantly office buildings the area was busy, during the day, though it was much quieter at night. Coffee shops along the street and several consulates on upper floors of nearby buildings were close to the scene as was the Queen Victoria shopping Centre comprised of mostly up market stores.

The Queen Victoria building was a grand building. Its presence on the block long site was preceded by a fresh food market that was built and operated in the early days of the settlement of Sydney, the early1800's. At one time the Queen Vic. as it was affectionately known faced the possibility of demolition, with its only substantial occupant at the time being the City of Sydney Library. The building that existed before its grand make over was bought up by overseas investors who refurbished the building. The building was turned from a general-purpose office building into a cathedral to retailing offering a selection of boutiques, cafes and other stores which were great for window shopping even if you could not afford to enter them. A beautiful building with a unique clock on its top floor memorialising some battle or another that provided a show on the hour, which played well to those people who travelled to the City of Sydney

Stores around the murder scene were generally still closed though some of the coffee places along the adjacent York Street were seeing some activity with the start-up of the breakfast trade. It was unlikely that anyone would have been working in any of the offices, shops or businesses that fronted onto Market or York Street, at this time of day.

The office buildings in the area as well as most other businesses were sure to be closed so early in the day. A bar and gym near the corner of York Street if they were operating could offer some potential witnesses.

Bus stops filled up much of York Street with only occasional buses coming and going at the time of the murder. The presence of people and action for the day was starting to pick up as Amy arrived at the scene as morning broke through the night. Light replacing dark on the same regular basis as it had done for time in memorial.

Amy reiterated her instructions to uniforms and her team who were all now at the scene. Three uniform police and her team were allocated to Amy's group along with two new detectives, who arrived at the scene shortly after Amy and Kalum arrived. Aerial Elmira and Johnathan Lewis-Brown were the new detectives completing the am AMY led "Check with the drivers on the light rail to see if they saw anything at that time of night if they operate on a Monday night," was the final instruction. She promised Ariel and Johnathan that she and Kalum would catch up with them later

The light rail, really a tram if you came for Melbourne or a trolley car if you knew San Francisco was originally a project of a state premier long since having left politics for a better paid and less strenuous job. It was a people mover which went from one end of the city to another. The city was well served by a circle of underground rail stations and above ground buses, but the light rail it was said would make Sydney an international city. Apparently, that was all that was needed to give Sydney an international look.

Though the light rail project had run well over budget and was two years late in its commencement it now worked effectively, if not efficiently. It was a short distance from the murder scene to the light rail tracks. Even so, it occurred to

Amy that it would be unlikely that the driver and only marginally less unlikely that any passengers had seen anything even if a carriage had come by at the right time.

Amy allocated the door knocking of an extended neighbourhood including the surrounding streets for a block each way. Even if anybody had not seen the crime they may have heard or seen something unusual.

'Don't hesitate to go upstairs in the buildings in the search area and ask at every business and of every resident if there was someone awake around when the shooting occurred." urged Amy though trying not to look to over enthusiastic in rallying the troops, which might betray her mixture of nervousness and excitement. However, her spirits had been lifted through her elevation to her new status, if only of a temporary nature. Amy now felt like she was ready for anything.

Amy and Kalum had read about the background of the new detectives, but this was their first meeting. A quick hello with a promise to catch up later without any suggestion as to when or where later might be.

Amy had read as much as possible. It seemed Aerial Elmira a new member of the division had been successful in passing her detective exam and was seen as an up and comer. She had been given an early transfer into the detective ranks and was involved in a rotation through the various squads. Her latest attachment had brought her to the homicide squad. Though she, held a master's degree Aerial could hold her own with most street police. She had already received acknowledgment for her breakthrough in a series of burglary cases where she had mapped the area where the burglaries had taken place and identified a list of possible local possible offenders. From the list she found the guilty person inside a week whereas others officers who had worked on the case previously had not turned upon anything in a month long investigation.

Johnathan Lewis-Brown caught the attention of Amy. She was sure that he had winked at her as he walked away. Maybe she was imagining it. Who was Johnathan Lewis-Brown? His file was unusual. S was a new recruit and had immediately made detective. There was an explanation that he had served as an investigating officer for the Commonwealth police. No details. He seemed to Amy to be moving in the circles that her brother, (location of whom was currently unknown), travelled.

8. Cameron Hazelwood – "eyewitness"

The eyewitness turned out to be one Cameron Hazelwood. He had been sleeping in in a doorway in the adjacent Queen Victoria building. 'I woke up when I heard the two people arguing. They were trying to be quiet but were making plenty of noise in doing it. I told the other cops who arrived at the scene what happened. "

'So, what were they arguing about', chimed in Kalum

"It was about money; it is always about money'. 'What is always about money", Amy broke in. 'Arguments in that street... the dead man, Harrison always met with people that owed him money at that location. I have heard him before collecting off people that owe him money. He is always well-spoken and pleasant until he has to deal with people who do not pay."

'Did he say why the other person owed him money'?

'It was about a loan", replied Hazelwood "The dead man had loaned money to the other person and wanted repayment. The other person did not have what he was meant to repay. He came up short. He wanted to work out a deal for him to settle in the future."

'Did you ever hear what this loan was for' Kalum asked.

"Harrison seemed to be bank rolling anything. I heard that some people had taken out loans to finance new businesses. Others wanted money to underwrite drug deals that sometimes did not go well. Once there was mention of

Street Cleaner

money for foreign nationals buying real estate. I have heard other meetings in the middle of the night between Harrison and other people but with no one I know.

He would say 'you accepted the money you have to manage the risks. It is not just me involved there are other investors who want you to pay. They act on recovery rather than talk about the money you have not paid.'

This time it was money to finance a deal where, not all the goods had arrived. Some deals where money was not repaid angered Harrison more than some other loans. However, when people did not pay on time Harrison wanted prompt fresh promises of payment with heavy penalties.'

All this was news to Amy and Kalum. It was clear that Harrison had well and truly folded the gambling business of his youth in the face of online gaming. He was now into the business of financing, a true lender of last resort.

Kalum broke the brief silence "so what happened when the customer said he could not pay what he owed on time?'

"They started to argue. The dead man and the person he was arguing with were interrupted by the shooter who came out of the dark from the top of the road. He walked up to Harrison and said you are "financing scum, the streets need to be cleaned of people like you". The other man started to run towards York Street. The shooter showed no interest in him. It was clear he was there for Harrison.

"The dead man tried to run, but the gunman was able to wound him and walked up to him as he tried to crawl away and shot him in the head. I ducked down and pretended to be asleep."

'What did the shooter look like?" Amy asked.

'He was big." Not great help Amy and Kalum concurred without saying anything. Amy followed up, 'Is there more?".

So were many people in the population. You did not need to take a Charles Atlas course these days. Many people were big in Sydney, not all of them professional wrestlers but a goodly number were in the security business of one type or another.

 "He had on a long black coat. The type people wear to the AFL in Melbourne". Not to suggest that AFL fans are all criminals or stand over people." The fashion was the same.

"He had what looked like the collar of a blue formal business shirt under the coat. I think he also wore a red tie, like he was going to work. It appeared briefly in the light of his phone, which shone in his pocket though he switched the light off quick. After the shooting the shooter walked into George street No traffic to slow him down" finished Hazelwood who was starting to look a little tired from his recounting of his adventure

"What about his face, his hands, his walk, his speech?' asked Kalum
Hazelwood went on. "His hands were big. I could not see any marks on them. It was too dark to see much detail. He spoke strongly, deeply, and decisively, using a natural voice. His face was not fully profiled in the light. The walk was almost a march I guess like a slow march, military style".

"Who was Harrison arguing with?' followed up Kalum.

"An easy question it was Eli Korobiete, who was the other man. I knew his wispy voice. A bit like someone speaking in a wind except his created his own wind."

Amy and Kalum exchanged glances. If it was Eli Korobiete, then instinctively they knew that the argument had to almost certainly be about payment of borrowed money. The money would likely be to underwrite a drug deal. Korobiete of an indeterminate Pacific Islander heritage was known as a middle level drug boss in Sydney's East. Rumour had it that he was extending his territory to the central west area and o the western area of Sydney around Parramatta. He would have needed money to increase his supply to cater for new clients as well as meet the demands of his existing clientele.

Maybe Korobiete's drug deal had gone wrong. Did his supplier take the money and run? Had the supplier had his merchandise seized by police, (though no big bust had been recorded of late) or stolen by another supplier, maybe the prices on the street were down if there had been an excess of supply? Whatever it was, though Amy, the deal looked like it had not gone to plan, which no doubt would have led to the meeting with Harrison. They were about to take a trip to the Eastern suburbs to track down Korobiete.

Kalum broke the silence with a question to the homeless man. "How can we be sure you are telling us the truth? Maybe you were the one that Harrison was meeting, and it all went wrong"

Indignantly Hazelwood put on a pathetic almost childlike voice, "Do I look like someone to whom Harrison would lend money?

So what were you doing here sleeping and how do you know so much about Harrison and his activities?

'I have not always lived on a street and fallen asleep in doorways. I was laid off. I began to spend the severance money I received travelling here and there. It was going too quickly so I hitch hiked while working here and there to get around the world. Then I decided I needed to plan for my future. I sold my house and put money into an investment/retirement fund, with a manager I have known all my life, who promise me he would get the best possible return on my investment. I did not hang onto more than I needed. But I miscalculated. I had not allowed myself enough money to live on so I decided to leave my money in the fund till I maximised my payout and live around the city for the last month or so.

A couple of weeks on the street have made me feel lost and broken, a bit like that program 'Rich and Homeless', the program where the children of rich families experienced homelessness. One of them rang his mother not sure of what to do being homeless. I feel a little bit the same.

In eight days, I will be of the age so I can get the money tax free and then I am moving on to a small but nice place somewhere on the south coast. A place down the coast with a water view where every day seems like a holiday."

Street Cleaner

A strange story maybe, but nothing further to be gained here thought Amy. "So where can we reach you if we need to go over some of your statement"?

"Around the town for eight more days and then I am off to where the sky meets the sea and where the sea meets the sand."

9. Ray Toller announces visitors for Eli Korobiete

Amy and Kalum left one of the uniforms to figure out where the sky meets the sea, and the sea meets the sand. Hazelwood's statement would be formally recorded and passed on to the team leader of the uniforms later in the day as well as being added to the case file, "the murder book."

They were now driving with Kalum at the wheel, towards Randwick to check whether Eli Korobiete was home.

"So being from the western suburbs, I am not fully up on the criminal hierarchy from the east. What is the run down on Korobiete?" asked Kalum.

Amy explained, "Korobiete is a middle level criminal. The worst we have got on him is that he was caught with undeclared income. The amount undeclared was around two hundred thousand dollars. His accountant said it was an error he made. The ATO gave the accountant a fine. Life goes on.

We know that he has provided protection and debt collection services around town. He has a close group of associates maybe better described as troops. None of them get in to fights or draw attention to themselves or Korobiete. Korobiete has apparently told his associates not to threaten anyone just to hint at what issues can occur if they do not comply with request for repayment or for stopping an activity. He picks people to be his associates based on how are well spoken they are, there physical fitness and training and the way they look after their appearance. Some, of his associates are university educated and all at least have diplomas or above. He wants a presentable and educated thinking work force. He provides housing for each of them and pays them well, so I believe.

It is thought that he dabbles in drugs but from afar. His associates have been caught with small amounts of amphetamines which have resulted in fines and an apology to the courts. Normally they claim that they have taken them off someone else to prevent self-harm. Witnesses have turned up saying they were saved by the actions of one of the associates of Eli Korobiete."

"Really" broke in Kalum. "He and his associates sound like 'great humanitarians'."

"It is a good story but the few times an associate has been caught for possession it seems like they were providing a sample of the load to some unknown. Anyway Eli and his associates try to keep their distance from the street drug dealers. It is suspected that he just puts up the money and monitors the outcome. He and his associates appear to only get involved when things don't go to plan," concluded Amy starting to shut her eyes, just for a moment of rest.

A few minutes later they pulled up at a small three-story block of units. Korobiete lived on the top floor of unit block on Alison Road. He had bought the block of six units some time back and had turned the two large units on the third floor into a single unit. The rest of the block was now rented out to associates of Korobiete. The renovations had been approved by council and carried out by a licensed builder. All building redesign was on record and legal.

Korobiete liked the area. Close to coffee shops and restaurants where he did his "business". He was also within walking distance to Royal Randwick where Eli spent his leisure time investing on horses when not otherwise working.

The purchase of the block of units had been a windfall for the previous owners. The units at the time were somewhere around the million-dollar mark each but each owner was offered, $1.4 million, or purchase of a similar unit in the area with $200,000 in their pocket without any legal fees. The sale resulted in about a half and half split. Half of the unit owners went for a similar unit elsewhere with the bonus payment. The other half took the higher than normal price with no agent fees or legal fees.

The block looked better than when Korobiete had bought it. The facade had been remodelled to give it a Roman look. Columns and a covering arch, all of which did nothing structurally, headed the short pathway to the door, along with bright selection of ground cover plants in a well-cared for small but bright garden plot. A vertical garden grew on the main wall of the building while high fences with discrete signs relating to mild but hurtful electrification appeared on the stone fences.

It was rumoured that the foyer and all the window glass had been replaced with one-way bullet-proof glass, though nobody knew for sure other than the glazier, who when asked by the media said he was "just running a small niche business and he did not want to discuss his clients and their needs with anyone."

Street Cleaner

The front door was security locked. The door looked more solid than most front doors. There was no mailbox except for a small hole in the wall. There were no unit numbers. Korobiete had all callers go through which ever of his associates was on duty.

A buzzing sound was heard when Kalum pressed a small intercom buzzer. After buzzing twice, a voice was heard on the intercom beside the door.

"How may I assist you today"?

"My name is Detective Inspector Any Whitelaw. With me is Detective Sergeant Kalum Menzies. We are here to speak to Mr. Korobiete"

"Can I advise Mr Korobiete, of the nature of the matter you wish to discuss?" returned the bodiless voice from the intercom"

"It is in regard to a murder investigation" responded Amy.

"Very well I will inform Mr. Korobiete of your presence and the matter at hand. Please enter the foyer and help yourself to coffee" the disconnected voice invited.

Amy and Kalum were buzzed in to find that the foyer was set up as a waiting room. There are no visible steps up to any upper floors. A coffee machine, coffee pods, cups, small plates, forks and a small fridge which would have revealed if it had been opened, three types of milk and a selection of fruit juices. A microwave to heat the Danish pastries plated and left on a small table. A television mounted on the non-glass wall switched on as they moved towards two small lounges. It was more like a waiting room than a foyer. Amy and Kalum sat without trying any of the Danish treats or drinks available.

Clearly there were things here to amuse Mr. Korobiete's visitors, which allowed for a long comfortable wait in the waiting room, if Mr Korobiete was delayed or chose to make visitors wait. No one to be seen.

"Inspector, Sergeant would you be good enough to hold your badges up to the camera in the right-hand corner of the room?

Amy and Kalum rose from their lounges without comment. The voice had come through a wall speaker. No visible door for entry beyond the waiting area

A minute late the door which was merged with the wall opened and a well-built bald man who appeared to be in the early to mid-thirties emerged. The bodiless voice was now a reality.

A momentary thought flashed through Amy's mind. The person dressed in dark trousers a white shirt and red tie would not be out of place as James Bond 007. Good looking and the age envisaged by Ian Fleming for the 007 with a license to kill (and to thrill). Amy's thoughts were wandering after the previous night outing to a crime scene and the 5:00AM start. The now bodied voice looked as if he had just finished getting ready for the day

"Thank you for waiting my name "is (James? thought Amy), Ray, Ray Toller," stated the newest entrant to the room. "I am sorry to keep you waiting. I hope you were comfortable. Mr. Korobiete can see you now. Would you be good enough to precede me up the stairs and wait at the door to the right?"

"So do you live here, Ray?" asked Kalum.

"I do live here when I am on duty. I am one of five associates of Mr. Korobiete, who stay here while on duty. There is always someone on duty in the house. Even when Mr. Korobiete leaves on business one of us will be on duty or if all the house associates are required to leave, with Mr. Korobiete one of the off-premises associates will come to the house on a temporary basis.

I have a flat nearby in another block owned by Mr. Korobiete. Please wait here and I will announce you. Mr. Korobiete will be with you in a moment. Again Amy and Kalum were in a holding bay awaiting an audience."

The hallway that normally would travel along the side of a floor of flats had been built in. Plans lodged for the development application to make changes to the building showed that the top floor two "pent house "units had been incorporated into a single living space. Ray walked through a large door and could be heard talking with another as unseen person.

Amy stood with Kalum outside the door for a short time. Ray reappeared within a minute and indicated that Amy and Kalum should follow him into a room and invited them to choose a chair each from one of the four beautifully upholstered chairs. In the far corner of the room sat Eli Korobiete.

He rose, smiled and extended his hand firstly to Amy and then to Kalum while at the same time asking if they would like anything to drink, coffee, water or tea, during which time Ray left the room.

The room seemed to be an anti-room to the rest of residence that would be suitable for meetings and relaxed entertaining. Casual coffee tables were near each chair with a central large coffee table. Heavy red drapes framed the single large window which looked out onto the street. Along the walls were open cabinets holding a variety of glass ware and wines along with what appeared to be awards recognising Korobiete or his business organisations for their contribution to or involvement in community activities. The floor was polished wood with a large white rug in the centre of the room. Another door was the opposite end of the room form where they had entered.

"Welcome", Korobiete started in his whispery windy voice, with enough of a positive facial expression to show that he seemed to mean it. He appeared to be truthful in his welcome or was a good actor working to a long-practiced script.

"Ray tells me you are investigating a murder".

Amy led off "James Harrison, who I believe is a business acquaintance of yours was murdered earlier this morning."

Everyone was silent while the statement seemed to hang in air, waiting till someone seemingly picked it up.

"You are right James and I do/did some business together from time to time. His murder, is not the one on the early news near York Street?"

"Yes it was. Harrison was shot twice and died at the scene. Have you conducted regular business with him?'

"From time to time, we have collaborated on various projects. If I had proposal and James feet it worthy then he often financed it. Sometimes he would assess the risk and get involved in making it happen with an agreed profit split. On other occasions he would put up money for an agreed return. On occasions, James had been not in position to join me in a new project.

'So you did business regularly,' said Kalum.

"I would say often rather than regularly. James had a good business mind. I understand he was currently managing funds for a consortium of cashed up people though I believe he contributed a substantial proportion of the funds himself. I again understand but cannot confirm that he was allowed an additional amount for managing the funds of others. I suspect as long as he achieved a require return that pleased other investors, they were happy, though he did mention once that they wanted him to have the same exposure for his funds that they faced. They felt it ensured his commitment to ensuring that projects financed, would succeed.

Street Cleaner

The business side of Eli Korobiete and James Harrison was a line of enquiry for another day by another group of police

"When did you see last see James Harrison"?

Everyone was quiet for a moment and did not move.

After thirsty seconds went by, Korobiete answered, "I saw James earlier this morning. It would appear that our meeting was not far from where he died."

"What was the meeting about?"

Kalum was now suddenly noticeably fidgety. Though Korobiete was answering the questions Amy was putting to him, Kalum thought his answers were not getting to the heart of the matter at any great speed. Amy knew it would take time. Korobiete would be fulsome in his answers with detail that may not matter possibly in an attempt to tire out and dry up the questioner.

Korobiete replied, "We had a meeting about funding for a project. The cash flow from the project had been slower than had been planned. I was negotiating with James to develop a new schedule for repayment of the loan. I accepted all the risk on this venture"

"It seems an odd place to meet, during the night in the middle of Sydney"

"It is an odd time, but James wanted to talk, last night. He said he had plans earlier and to meet him in the city as he had another appointment close by"

"Was anyone else there?

"A man did walk up to James and spoke to him just as the meeting was concluding. I took it as my time to leave as the meeting was over. I was cold and wanted to get to my car quickly."

So what did the other man say? "James Harrison? James replied yes. That is all I heard"

"Nothing else, no further parts of the conversation, no other sounds...?'

"Nothing"

"Mr. Korobiete, did you see anyone else around other than the man who approached Harrison?"

Korobiete paused for a few seconds. Was he wondering where this was going? Did he believe that there might be a witness?

"No one"

"We have someone who saw you at the murder scene and said the discussion, negotiation was heated. Did you leave the meeting before it was over? The other man disturbed the meeting. Were you arguing with Harrison rather than negotiating?"

"Well, you are right. There were some heated words. When discussing money which is overdue then there can be some heated words exchanged. However, I would still characterise the meeting as a negotiation. Big boys, big dollars"

Kalum began shifting in his chair. He hated when people started a sentence with "Well"…It reminded him of a former senior politician who started the answer to every question asked of him in parliament. It seemed to Kalum that Eli Korobiete was a politician criminal.

Amy went out on a bit of a limb. "Isn't it true the man who interrupted your negotiation was employed by you Mr. Korobiete to eliminate the problem of James Harrison as your 'negotiation' was going badly?"

"Inspector, you know that isn't true otherwise we would have left here and be talking at the station. I did not know or see the man who approached James. He had on a dark coat. That is all I saw. I turned away and took off back to my car as he walked up. I think we are done now."

The welcome seemed to be over.

"Mr. Korobiete we are likely to want to talk to you again. Please advise us if you are going to be absent from Sydney for more than a few days" added Kalum for his first and last words during the meeting, while handing his card to Korobiete.

"Always" said Korobiete rinsing form his chair. "Inspector, Sergeant I have some other matters to see to, Ray will show you out"

Street Cleaner

At which point the concealed door opened and Ray walked in while Eli Korobiete, disappeared through another concealed door at the other end of the room.

10. The junior attachés, the bar cleaner and other people – "all saw something".

As they drove away from the Korobiete residence, Amy expressed her satisfaction to Kalum that Korobiete admitted to being at the scene though of course not disclosing anything he may have seen. It verified the story of the so called homeless man. It was time to talk to any other witness that had been turned up by the uniforms but maybe something to eat and coffee first. It was now mid-morning with breakfast a memory. They pulled over a service station and ordered.

Driving again, Kalum remained quiet apart from noises indicating attention to what Amy was saying but without comment. Silence filled the car till after a time Amy asked:

"What is on your mind Kalum?"

"So far we have met a maybe retrenched person living on the street so he claims he can maximise his retirement income. An enforcer who acts like a butler and a crim who acts like a sophisticated businessman, in the case of the murder of a university educated loan shark. We have encountered a strange assortment of people so far. No apparent progress in solving the crime"

Any wasn't sure about Kalum's characterisation of the people involved in the case so far. Ray Toller had a conviction for a low level possession but had produced a witness to say that Ray had taken the drug from him to protect the user from himself. Eli Korobiete had never been arrested let alone convicted of anything. The homeless man had given a strange explanation for his presence at the scene. Amy had to agree that the case was throwing up a strange assortment of people but so did many cases.

Arriving back, the office was now quiet with detectives working on cases on the streets. Those officers still present were researching on the net, writing reports or examining evidence in their cases found in their murder book.

Superintendent John Chapman came by as Amy finished two cheese and tomato toasties, they had picked up on the way in. Warm and filling, not heavy, with a large Latte all offered a pleasant sensation after the cold of the early start. Something to allow Amy to push onto a late lunch

"Amy" said Chapman "we have the names of the other witnesses to be interviewed, Bible has the details. "

Amy summoned Kalum who was finishing his second cup of coffee and seemed to be enjoying the several premade sandwiches he had picked up. Chapman repeated himself apparently to extend the conversation "You need to see Bible. He has a list of people tuned up by the uniforms". Apparently, he has some interesting people to interview." More 'interesting' people thought Kalum who betrayed his thoughts to Amy with his unconvincing twisted face smile.

Bible was a long serving acting sergeant who had been a detective for many years. Like Kalum he had come from the west as a constable and was waiting to be made Sergeant permanently. As happy as he portrayed, Bible was not to be underestimated. He was drawn to anger when he saw suffering inflicted by felons, particularly on the innocent.

Bible got his name as he attended a large Christian Church at the Hills area where he now lived with his family. Bible quoted or often amended, or misapplied bible texts to fit a situation, at least as he saw it.

"Bible, you have many wonderful people for us to spend the afternoon talking with?

"Indeed, I do Amy. It is time for you both to go together onto the highways and the byways."

"The reference enquired Amy?" sure that it was not a quote from the Book"

"No reference my friend just a turn of phrase to describe the delight you will experience when meeting the several people I have for you to see.

Bible his usual cheerful self, started to run through his short list. "On Market Street there are various consulates. Brazil, Spain and France are in the same building. Some of the people work all night." he said with a peculiar grin or was it a smirk on his face.

"An attaché from each of the Spanish and the French consulates were having a little private party in the French consulate. They are Mademoiselle Adelle Veil, from the French Consulate and Miss Cristina Torres, from the Spanish consulate. I rang their workplace, and both are working today. They each told their bosses that they wanted to work back to get ahead on an upcoming project. Their bosses agreed and they were working very late last night.

At a bar up the street the bar manager said he was unsure of when his cleaner had started work but it the cleaner left a note letting the owner know that there was action about last night. The cleaner is a contractor and changes the order of jobs he needs to complete some nights. Apparently, it breaks the monotony of the work. He does the jobs each night for city businesses and has to be finished with these premises by 6:00 AM. He may have started at the club, "Market on York", obviously a play on the street names. The owner rang the cleaner and he said he would be there around 1:00AM but was unavailable before then. "

"Helpful", what is his name broke in Kalum"? who now appeared to be keen to get out of the office and on their way, or was he edgy about some other thing that was not apparent?

Bible continued unruffled by a young man who he knew wanted to be away from his current location. "The cleaner calls himself Waleed Taha. Apparently, he has a much longer name but uses the normal first and a truncated second name in Australia. Nothing is known on him. His address in Redfern is vacant land. The address was a building site with new flats said to be under construction. We don't know if he ever lived at the address he gave his clients. His mail goes to a post box but not at a post office, a specialised mail collection service. As I said he will be back at 1:00 AM tomorrow morning if you feel, like a late night/early morning."

The prospect for Amy of another early morning/late night was not appealing. If she and Kalum stayed up till 1:00 then it was likely to be a twenty-hour day. Maybe some time off later today and back tonight was the way to be fresh to question the possible witness.

"Anyone else?

"Some of the premises require return visits. No one was there when the uniforms called. Some people were in but were unsure as to whether other people had been working late as they had not been there at night. Most promised to call back later in the day.

One person appeared to be not sure where he was. He said he was in the office late. Said he had not heard anything. The uniforms thought he was hiding something. His name is Anosmia Smith, which I guess is an unusual name. He was at a company called "Furniture with you" apparently some sort of furniture fit out place for businesses. Here is his address. The new detectives could have another look at him". Bible concluded his information by handing Amy a piece of paper.

"Safe travel." wished Bible as Amy and Kalum started heading for the door. Back to the murder scene with the first stop being the two young attachés.

Amy and Kalum arrived promptly at the building housing the consulates that fronted onto Market Street. Amy took the Cristina Torres from the Spanish embassy and Kalum was to question Adelle Veil from the French embassy.

Street Cleaner

Plans for separate interviews were soon abandoned. The two attachés had their own plan as to how the interview was to go. They had explained to their respective bosses what they had possibly seen and that the police might be calling.
Amy and Kalum found the same response from each of the women. Each of them said they were happy to meet with the police but wanted to do it in a relaxed environment away from their offices and would only talk if they were interviewed together.

The foursome convened at one of the many coffee shops in the Queen Victoria building. Amy paid for four coffees and a small serving of cookies. Though not satisfied with this arrangement she had acquiesced and lead off the interview, "So why were you working at the time of the murder?"

Cristina Torres led off, "We were working on a project for the consulates. They wanted us to finalise a plan for a joint approach to the Open Sydney day later in the year. Other consulates and trade organisations have been open in the past, so we thought we should be as well."

Amy knew of Open Sydney. Once a year Open Sydney allowed the public into buildings in which they would not normally be allowed. Most of the buildings had a story attached to them. Most businesses opened their buildings as a form of promotion. Amy on one occasion with her date for the day, had wandered through solicitors chambers, a bank building with façade from another century with internals from today and buildings which had hard to believe stories

Cristina went on," Unlike the people at Hong Kong House our consulates do not have the same architectural or historical interest in their surroundings. Though Open Sydney is some months away our managers thought given we are in the same building we should get together and come up with a cultural proposal that would suit both of our consulates."

"It is still late to be working?' chimed in Amy given the crime had occurred early in the morning

"It is true" said Adelle Veil in what proved to be a rich French accent, "we had completed most of the proposed plan but we have become friends and since we have been working on this project we have been talking of getting a flat together though we would need consulate permission from both consulates. We had enjoyed some French wine, to see whether it should be part of our exhibit. It helped to pass the time and we had slept a little but were awake at the time of the shooting."

As if they were a tag team Cristina continued the story." Yes, we heard two people shouting and went to the window onto Market Street. Two men were arguing. It was not clear as to what they were arguing about, but the word money came up several times. A third man approached the scene, with one of the two who had been in discussion taking off quickly. There was a short conversation between the man who was left and the other person who had arrived at the scene of the argument. Then the new man on the scene shot the man who died. We ducked in case they saw us though the room we were in was dark."

 "And then," Cristian paused Amy gave an encouraging look to Adelle, Cristina's tag team partner who went on.

Street Cleaner

"We stood up a little to get a view outside. There was a second shot. We ducked down but still could see. We saw the man who had been shot on the ground. The tall person who fired the shots was standing over him as he was picking up something. He paused for a second and then walked away, discarding a piece of paper on the ground."

Kalum who had been listening more alertly than Amy expected chipped in, "A piece of paper?"

"Yes" continued Adelle obviously forgetting to tag in Cristina.

"He walked towards George Street, discarding a piece of paper that was blown after him as he approached the corner."

"Did you do anything after that?" interjected Amy cutting Kalum off from pursuing the paper chase further.

Cristina now tagged in, "I rang my friend, a male friend and asked what to do. He said he would ring the police. I was concerned with questions about us working so late. Also having to explain immediately what we saw. We needed to take it all in and make sure we understood what we had seen. We needed to process it."

Ah, Amy thought, the processing of what we see. Everyone seems to need to process everything, place it in some way so that it fits with their understanding of the world, or they need to revise understandings to fit a new event into held understandings. Interviews often stalled with the need for processing facts. Why the need for processing? Could we not just have people tell us what they saw?

"What about this piece of paper you mentioned. Did you see anything on the paper"? "It looked like a number, maybe a two", the two attaches mumbled together.

There was nothing more to be gained from these two witnesses at the moment. They were asked to advise the police if they were going more than a hundred kilometres from Sydney which they readily agreed to do. Business cards exchanged and the meeting was over.

As they left the building Amy messaged Bible about the mystery piece of paper and asked him to arrange for a search of garbage picked up in the area even if it meant searching through a processing facility or search at the tip. Bible's reply was as normal was short and to the point. "On it, it certainly does not sound like a word from God."

She smiled to herself and messaged her boss and relayed a summary of their efforts so far today, including the "lead" on the mysterious piece of paper dispensed with by the shooter. She suggested as it was now after 1:00 PM that she and Kalum take some time off till 6:00PM when teams would meet and summarise their day and then work on till the 1:00AM meeting with the apparently "homeless" cleaner.

The reply was short and to the point "See you at 18:00".

Amy and Kalum had discussed in the past the European system for recording time. They agreed the European timing system is so easy to understand none of this AM and PM. Her mind was tired. Amy's thoughts were wandering to the irrelevancy of measuring time.

Street Cleaner

Surely regardless of the hour it was time for a break.

11. The Cleaner settles in.

Renting the apartment had been easier than expected. A call from a public phone at the airport was all it took. The need to rent an apartment quickly before leaving on a supposed interstate trip, the offer of payment of three months' rent in advance paid by credit card on the phone in a name other than the Cleaner's real name had been readily accepted.

The agent or was it the landlord said he would get a cleaner to tidy up. The Cleaner declined "I have my own cleaning approach', a comment that surely confused the disengaged voice on the other end of the phone, but he readily accepted that his new renter did not need a cleaner. After all, thought our killer, I am a cleaner.

The lease dispatched to a post office box, signed, and returned several weeks later with a further three months' rent, for six in advance, made for a happy landlord, agent and tenant.

Who said you need identification. A fake license and fake references were far outweighed by the upfront rental payment on an apartment in a difficult to rent area. The law is bent by many people thought the Cleaner. It was clear to him that it was money over morals.

"Virgilan", (the Cleaner enjoyed these meaningless pseudonyms), yes that is "Vir.gil.an (spelling it out to ensure there was a clear impression of the name he had left with the real estate agent). Always keeping his head down to ensure identification from CCTV was difficult..... "I want to be able to take up residence immediately upon my return. It may be between one and three weeks before I move in. I will only be there few days per month as I pass through………" It had been an easy deal to make

Renting a mailbox was equally as easy. The private post box business was happy to accept an application by post. Mailbox keys left in the box closed but not locked. No mail was expected or likely welcomed

The gun had been easy to find. The city had many places where a gun and a plentiful supply of ammunition could be bought. The Southwest area of the city in particular offered many opportunities to purchase a weapon.

Local drug lords also ran a profitable enterprise in supplying illegal guns, many of which were made illegal after the "Port Arthur massacre," in Tasmania where thirty-five people were killed as well eighteen injured by a lone gunman, Martin Bryant, a wealthy but deranged killer, who was sentenced to thirty five life terms.

The Cleaner knew in general terms who to reach out to for a gun because of his past work. No one recognised him with a prominent artifice scar, contact lenses changing eye colour, a short beard and an unusual ensemble while going by the name of Christopher Baracus, a first name he always liked, and a last name borrowed from an old television show.

There had been little nervousness for the Cleaner in establishing a new identity, the apartment, the post office box and purchase of gun had been easy and for a moment the ease of his deception gave pause for second thoughts as to whether someone may have been able to identify him. But such thoughts were fleeting.

The streets of Sydney were strewn with dirt. The dirt was those people who polluted society, the financiers, the dealers, and the tax cheats. Society required a cleaner. He was the Cleaner.

The courts failed to permanently clean the streets. A temporary time away for those that were caught and proven guilty and then they are back returning to old habits or taking up new habits they had learned in the "school of prison". Even though people were caught who had transgressed the norms of society some did not do any prison time. Witnesses would suddenly not testify. Community orders and large fines often used as punishment turned out to be impotent. Incomplete investigations by the police would let some of the unconvicted criminals escape any penalty.

Now, he thought I need a relaxing bath. The body of the cleaner, cleaned and visible in the half-light of a lamp from an adjacent room of his well-turned out town house in a northern seaside suburb of Sydney. No need to use the rented inner city flat yet. The comforting thought of a future job well done quickly brought sleep.

However, any peaceful sleep was disturbed by constant wakening. Dreams of his the stabbings of two years past interjected his comatose state. Another of a father that had died seeking justice streaked across the mind. The echoing of possible future words of those in authority. '...Just a vigilante, no better than those who were killed.'

Street Cleaner

A two-year pause, give or take. He was now convinced to start his mission in earnest. He was now home in his country. He had tried to eliminate his desire to right society outside the law but the steps he had taken to cleanse himself of the desires to "clean up" were doomed to failure. His role as a "righter" of wrongs dominated his thinking. He thought of him as a self-proclaimed patriot with a mission.

Eventually the body of the Cleaner relaxed, his mind began to switch off a he recalled his shower, the warmth of the water and the lather of the body wash enable him to drift off, with one final thought.

A vigilante – maybe. Certainly a cleaner. He was the one who would be crowned the Street Cleaner.

12. Amy her dream shop – and the trolley man

With around five hours to go before a return to duty, Amy had time for some shopping that badly needed to be done and a couple of hours sleep for what might be an all-nighter.

The trip to home was a shorter one at this time of the day than in peak hour. A quick trip to the major shopping centre, with a good selection of stores without the inner-city bustle was available on the way home with almost always plentiful parking.

Parking on the roof she saw one of the unseen people of society, the trolley man. One of those people like the pamphleteer letter boxing leaflets and catalogues the trolley man (or woman) was an anonymous person carrying out an anonymous job.

The trolley person was someone that people smiled (or growled) at, or completely ignored. Not a person that most people are likely to remember. He or she collected trolleys as shoppers off loaded their purchases into their cars. Someone to yell about with derision as if they were a non-entity when no trolleys were available or the available trolleys were not to a customer's liking.

She had stopped to talk to a trolley man on another day. He recounted stories of assistance required of him to off load wheelchairs, requests to fix a car that would not start as well as more than one request for a trolley to be used for non-shopping purposes. "They are used as walkers by the aged.

Street Cleaner

The small trolleys are just the right height for a walker as well as being useful for shopping. It saves getting the walker out of the car."

Who were these trolley men and women? Why do they take this job? The trolley man I had spoken to previously had told me he was formerly a teacher.

He told of his plight "The state government withdrew funding and put-up fees. Many people could no longer afford to enrol at the school where I was teaching. Less students' means fewer teachers were needed. I took the retrenchment package. I could have competed for one of the few jobs retained... But I did not like the way the system was going so I left."

"I have met some interesting colleagues in the job. A man named Tyesha had come to Australia from Japan, set up a Japanese restaurant only to go out of business with the high Sydney inner city rents taking him to the wall resulting in a loss of $500K. Brienne came from Europe where he had a good job as a train driver to join family in Australia. He said to me, "Now I push trolleys for base rate. It is work and I need to work."

Amy made her way to the travellator and started the journey to one of the supermarkets found in the centre. As she perused items she saw two older men who seemed to be wandering in the shop. They looked a little aimless walking the aisles searching for something, which whine found and purchased possibly gave them some reason to justify their existence.

Street Cleaner

Amy's shop consisted of the same style of wondering but with a little more purpose. She picked up goods as she went from aisle to aisle. Do I need coffee? Apples or the sliced pineapple? Maybe some of both. Those pre-packaged meals, not the frozen ones, sped up dinner and meant it was quicker from stove to plate to lounge. Five would be good.

Amy was not in a mood to concentrate on anything but the case as she toured the aisles rather than being an intense shopper with a list. The case would reappear in her mind when the six o'clock meeting occurred and when she attended the late night meeting with the bar cleaner - Waleed Taha.

For some reason, as she came to the store prepared salads, she thought of her mother. Her mother Angela lived in the city of culture and food to south. Well, that was how Angela had described Melbourne to Amy, again and again and again. The flat that Angela occupied was in South Yarra one of the inner suburbs of Melbourne on the Sandringham line. It amused Amy how Melbourne station staff described their lines by specific names whereas in Sydney lines were described in general terms such as, western suburbs, northern suburbs, city circle etc.,

Amy's mother Angela had been a widow for the last eight years and had bought what she described as the snug two-bedroom unit in which she lived after Amy's father had died. She had consciously decided to move to Melbourne, a place she always described as being superior to Sydney. "It is easy to get to the city by train, tram or even bus for theatre and to enjoy city shopping and city fairs", Angela crowed to Amy every time they discussed their respective living arrangements.

She had an open invitation for Amy and her brother Brett to visit and stay but always pleaded poor health when it was suggested she visit her children in Sydney. "Darling the trip to the airport, the flight and the entry to Sydney is just too much. I can't travel that far." Yet she travelled on at least two cruises each year often leaving from Sydney "yes but everything is taken care of for me the pickup, time in lounge, carrying the bags, and on and on she went.

Probably better to have her in Melbourne. There would be constant scrutiny of meals eaten, men met and the hazards of the job as well as the constant comment on the lack of grandchildren. It was good to have my mother at least a day long trip away.

Amy thought of Brett who she had not seen for months. Amy thought of her brother who had been a former policeman who left because he became disillusioned. Brett had come to believe that the "system" favoured the crim's' against the police. I wonder how he is going as a private detective. The agency he joined on exiting the force was a positive step, well at least that was what he had said when I saw him last.

He now felt that he did not have to pretend he was catching the guilty who managed to move in and out of the legal system with apparent ease. He descried what he did now as silly cases. "Who is seeing who behind the back of someone else, occasional industrial secrets that people thought had been stolen, the apparent though not always real assumption that money had been taken or misused – but if you find anything don't inform the police."

Amy worried about Brett. He was a young person who had been on the move in the NSW police. He had worked part time previously for the Australian Federal Police, (AFP) on researching money trails to possible terrorists or criminal organisations. He had had been approached be the (AFP) to become a permanent member of staff but decided he would move back from Canberra where he had completed a university degree in finance and data mining back to Sydney to enlist in the NSW police. His skills and knowledge were put to good use. He was paid at a rate much higher that his rank as a constable. Some early wins had been offset by what he said were, "criminals going free in a biased criminal system".

 It was worrying to Amy that when she had last seen Brett some six months ago Brett described the nature of justice found in the ancient concept of the "Star Chamber". Real justice said Brett without fabrication of evidence and incessant appeals, swift and sure.

Amy had read about the Star Chamber which started in England in the late 15th century and probably ended in the mid-17th century. The Star Chamber was set up to ensure that people who were socially or political prominent would be judged based on the facts not on their position. Brett saw this approach as different from the society in which he which he worked. Wealth or a name could affect judgments in the normal courts where the court may not convict because of a person's position or a harsh judgement was avoided through the wielding of influence or the exchange of money.

Street Cleaner

The Star Chamber had been established to ensure that the guilty among the elite would be treated as if they were people who lacked wealth, standing or substance. Over time the Star Chamber became an excuse to abuse the court's power and make arbitrary decisions. The use of arbitrary "justice" was proposed by commentators in current times as the answer to the supposed lack of legitimacy of any court's proceedings where anyone believed the verdict to be incorrect.

Brett believed the concept of a 'Chamber" system of justice was an approach to be embraced. He applauded the idea if a 'higher "court which addressed what he saw as perceived wrongs. "If a Star Chamber could be introduced it could deal with those people, criminals, felons, who were guilty but crept away from the legal system largely unscathed.

Amy was pleased when he took out his private investigation license and turned what was initially a casual job into a fulltime job. After six months he was earning thirty per cent more than his former police salary. He had seemed happy with his job when she had seen him last but still harboured resentment for what he said were the perceived inadequacies of the current justice system.

"I need to catch up with him, mouthed Amy. I am still worried about his state of mind and silence between us does not necessarily mean it is 'golden".

"Amy"? Is someone calling me? I'm in a dream, I need to wake up and get home. A face she knew came into view.

13. The Cleaner - a tough day

The day at his day job work had been hard. Concentration had been jarred by the thoughts of the death of the previous night and the over whelming joy of starting his self-assigned mission of cleaning the streets

The day had ended. A day of work was over. Watching the markets in his spare time and attending to the needs of his stressful job made for a normal but tiring day after such an active and long night. The Cleaner poured his preferred type of wine into a glass. Not a connoisseur. It was a bottle of red wine... Not his favoured brand but palatable all the same.

Back at home the Cleaner surveyed the electronic news to see what had been written about his 'cleaning spree'. There was the mention of the death of Harrison. Shot in a city street late at night. Speculation as to whether Harrison knew his attacker given his attacker and that was why the killer had been able to the closet him. How true that was, though Harrison did not have time to register that fact. There was a brief mention of the recent death of "Sparrow Green" and whether the two deaths were connected.

'They certainly were." the Cleaner informed himself.

It was good to be home. The town house provided a convenient place to relax and recuperate, big enough for the Cleaner, but this "home" was of lesser importance than his new "profession".

Was it right or was to wrong for him to clean the streets. He again debated with himself the nature and value of his mission. The courts failed to provide tough penalties. Some people went uncharged. Crimes went unsolved. A touch of conscience when a life is gone but if the erasure of this life stops others losing theirs to a pursuit of crime or to drugs where some of the victims had a living death, tormented by minds which had long ceased to function as an informed human being. Surely a great good has been served, when the purveyor of living death whether directly or indirectly has been eliminated.

The Cleaner suddenly thought of his father now long gone. A father that believed that the system was sound but then found it did not provide the punishment deserved by the many that did wrong. Those people who failed to live as civilised people, who caused others to stumble, to die, and to live a living hell. People developed their own morals and ethics, outside the norm of society. Their own code of ethics developed where they believed that society was there for them not to serve it. Society was there to serve the criminal the perpetrator. When society did not provide what they needed, they took it. They removed obstacles, people that were in their way.

The Cleaner found he was sweating. What would his father have said of his campaign to clean the streets if he was here now? Would he have seen it as, right? Was the removal of street criminals just?

A cool breeze came through the window cooled his brow and disturbed his thinking.

Street Cleaner

The murder, his murder of Harrison was the second story on the Cleaner's news service. Another middle-eastern bombing was the subject of the lead story.

Why number two? It wasn't for glory but they did not and would not take the "street cleaning" as seriously as the Cleaner. The streets rid of another criminal. They had not seemed to notice the signature now left at the two murder scenes. Never mind, it was the service rendered to society rather than the signature that was important. Lack of recognition did not stop the Cleaner acting.

The eyes of the Cleaner slipped to another part of the electronic news. A white-collar criminal that had served three years in gaol for fraud was being released.

"Angela Bates convicted embezzler has been released from jail on parole. Bates, a solicitor, had been convicted of stealing money from a trust fund that she was meant to invest on behalf of her clients. She had been convicted of misappropriation of funds. Bates had used the funds to speculate on overseas share markets apparently with no success and had decided to recoup losses from the fund by a arranging for a professional gambler to win back the lost funds through gambling activities. However, the gambler absconded with the money she was given.

Bates is claimed to have lost some $25million of the money entrusted to her. Two of her clients committed suicide once they had found out that they had been wiped out. Bates is disqualified as a solicitor. She is never to be reinstated

Street Cleaner

In a statement read to the waiting media she said 'I am sorry about the past. I tried hard for these people to recoup their funds, but I had bad luck". Bates, has served eight years of a ten year sentence.

Bates is now living with her daughter having lost her house and other assets. She is to report to her parole officer once a week.

The Cleaner looked at the picture of the bookish woman. Bates was a minor criminal in the world of crime but still someone who caused others loss. She caused the loss of lives of the innocent. Filth on the streets thought the Cleaner that needs to be eliminated.

Her new home was in a leafy suburb, not far from the beach where he lived. Was the $25M the full extent of the loss? The Cleaner considered Ms. Bates and added her name to a growing of vermin to be eliminated.

14. A chance meeting

"Amy, Amy".

Amy had cleared her thoughts of her family. Shopping complete she have arrived at the car. Eventually Amy fully realised that someone was calling her.

Looking around and at first, I don't see anyone familiar. Then I notice a face which I have seen recently. A new face to me but one I have seen recently. Is that Johnathan Lewis-Brown calling?

The person calling is in fact Johnathan Lewis-Brown.

"Hi Amy I heard in the meeting room you lived near here. I have moved into the area. I had decided to take a shower and pick up some takeaway to eat before travelling back into the meeting. I am glad I caught you. I should tell you that when you rang in, Bible arranged for the garbage to be captured that came from the bins on the street before it got dumped as land fill. He pulled Aerial and I off the door to door and put us on photographing what appeared to be key items of rubbish. The rubbish from bins around the murder scene is currently being held separately at the city refuse centre, the dump. There will be a slide show of the various items we found at the meeting, but I think we have found what was discarded."

"Johnathan", Amy said now steadying herself from the unexpected intrusion "what did you find?'

"There was variety of mainly destroyed written items. However, there was a single sheet of paper that appeared to have been carefully prepared. It was a single sheet with the Number 2 in the centre. It had a header which read 'Cleaning the streets permanently' and a footer that read 'Page two of 2'

The rest of the garbage was mainly wrappers, food scraps and some documents which had been destroyed. This was the only page still intact though covered in the residue from scraps in the bin."

So our junior attachés had seen a piece of paper dropped by the tall man, thought Amy.

"I suppose there are no useable prints on the paper?'

"Just smudges which were not useful for identification."

"Why the number 2, what does it signify? The cleaning the streets permanently, sounds like a moralistic killer who has some sort of cleaning idea, or not?" Amy mused thinking out loud.

"I guess the obvious possibility is that he has killed someone else. This could be his second victim." responded Johnathan to a question that was close to surfacing in Amy's mind but not yet asked.

"It does seem that way. It could be as simple as you say. It is obvious but sometimes the obvious is what it is meant to be. Something obvious, to give people a message, to give us a message. So, Johnathan, you said you lived close by?" said

Amy determined change tack to let her mind rest from the case so she would be fresh for the meeting and later interview with the bar cleaner

"I live two suburbs further south. I wanted to be close to the job but not to close and here I have a bonus of being near the beach. I have a small unit I am renting till I can decide where I want to live. I sold a house that I bought in Canberra while I was in the army and wanted to settle somewhere on the northern beaches."

"You live alone?'

"Yes I have been too tied up with past work to form any sort of relationship."

Why had Amy asked this? He was attractive and had joined the force after being an Army officer. We seem to be about the same age maybe he is a little older. He had said he had stints in the army and I think he has been in the AFP. He came straight into the force as a Detective.

I wonder what he did before to come into the force as a detective. Stop- she was just trying to get to know this new detective.

Johnathan awoke Amy who had seemed to lapse into a dream like state "I should let you know that I know your brother Brett."

Her attempt to get to know this new detective drove her back to thinking about her family with a belt.

Street Cleaner

"I met Brett when I was on secondment from the Army to the (AFP). Brett and I were investigating the leaking of sensitive military information. He was great. We got on well"

Amy was taken aback at meeting someone who knew Brett. He had not talked much about the people he had met. This maybe a chance to find out more about how Brett before he joined the force. Amy was more worried now about her lack of contact with Brett.

"Johnathan, can we discuss this later. I want to clear my mind and catch a short sleep before we meet at 6:00. Can we get together later in the week? I have not met many of Brett's friends."

They parted smiling at each other. Did I just invite Johnathan on a date?

15. Bible calls "Order, quieten down."

"Order, quieten down." These were the first words of the six o'clock meeting. Amy hoped that others had found out something worthwhile. At the moment all they had were pieces.

The meeting was to review two high profile murder investigations. There could have been more cases discussed but now the two high profile cases were those before the media, the commissioner and the minister.

Meeting together to review each other's cases was a normal practice. It also allowed people to be up to date if there needed to be re-deployment of staff from one case to another. Cross fertilisation and new minds from other investigations allowed for new ideas to be developed or to look at things differently. Amy and Kalum's case was to come first.

Quiet came quickly. Bible, when he yelled had that impact on a group.

"Let's make a start. A minute wasted can never be reclaimed. Amy and Kalum were interviewing our witnesses on the Harrison case. A report please."

As Kalum started to put up pictures from his computer onto a screen and list people and their connections on a white board, Amy ran through their interviews. First up Cameron Hazelwood the apparently temporarily homeless man, who had stated from what he had heard that meetings in the middle of the night were apparently not unusual for Harrison. He had identified the voice of the man with who Harrison was arguing before the shooting as Eli Korobete. However Hazelwood could not identify the shooter. Hazelwood had stated that the shooter had said "you are financing the scum of the streets that need to be cleaned of people like you.' The shooter walked towards George Street when he left.

Next came their meeting with Eli Korobete and the presence of one of his associates Ray Toller. Korobete had agreed that he was with Harrison before he was shot. The meeting which, Hazelwood had characterised as turning into an argument was about the repayment funds for a project where the goods had not arrived. Mr Korobete was non-committal regarding the nature of the project. He claimed that the meeting had been disturbed by a tall person, who addressed Harrison by name, though Harrison did not seem to know the man. Korobete said he did not see or hear the shooting and left the murder scene quickly,

Their report then turned to the junior attachés, Adelle Veil and Cristina Torres. They each worked for their respective consulates and were cooperating on a planned display for Open Sydney. Apparently they had struck a friendship and had asked to work together on the project. They had been drinking and slept for a while but were sure but were aware when the heard shouting outside. When they looked out the window and saw two men arguing, Harrison and Korobete, when a third man walked up. One of the men left the scene quickly- Korobete.

Street Cleaner

Then the new arrival appeared to say something to the remaining man and then shot him. Both attaches ducked down but kept looking from a kneeling position. They saw and heard the second shot. As with Hazelwood they said the shooter walked form the scene towards George Street, having retrieved something from the ground. We assume this was the shell casings. They stated they felt concerned for their safety, so a male friend was rung who made the 000 call.

Veil and Torres the names of the witnesses also gave us the lead on the discarded item, which Johnathan Lewis-Brown and Aerial Amira will bring us up to date on.

Waleed Taha was to be interviewed. He is a cleaner in a club up the street from the crime scene. He works at night but does not live at his registered address. Apparently, he has various jobs around town. The manager of the bar at the corner of York and Market we spoke to said he always does a good job. He gets his work through recommendation. The manager at the club has a word out on the street that we want to meet him tonight. We are meeting him later, much later.

Amy's final comments were greeted with muted laughter. The thought of extending an already long day into a late night was something everyone always wanted to avoid. Much better it is someone else than me.

The laughter subsided when Bible announced that the meeting needed to keep going. The hour was late and would only be later if we spent valuable time laughing at the plight of our colleagues, which brought out a new series of stifled laughs.

Bible followed up the presentation with an initial forensic report. "Cause of death is two bullets to head. Harrison did not suffer in that death was all but instantaneous.

I am sure you are a happy about that. (A few more small chuckles from around the room)

Harrison did not have any apparent illnesses of conditions except for enlarged heart. He was lender of last resort with a big heart. (The absence of even a chuckle indicated attempts at humour now seemed misplaced)

Blood Tests etc. to come."

Bible finished his news from the autopsy and turned his frown into a smile

"Now please welcome our new recruits, Aerial Elmira, and Johnathan Lewis-Brown who have had a busy first day."

A small round of applause hailed Aerial, who though a newbie led off with a succinct and interesting summary of her and Johnathan's activities. Aerial announced that their door to door had not turned up any more witnesses. The man of mystery who had the unusual name of Anosmia Smith was not at the premises where he was earlier today. The place where he had been found looked deserted. It had been cleaned out. We were coming back to do some follow up on him when Bible called and redeployed us to rubbish.

Street Cleaner

'Johnathan?

"Aerial is right" Johnathan took over. "We were redeployed to catch the garbage which was on the street at the time of the shooting. We tracked down the truck on the way to the tip. Searching through the rubbish we found many curious items, old vases, food scraps, a dead dog, and various pieces of paper. The piece of paper that may be related to the case had the number two on it: "

Johnathan lit up the drop-down screen with an enlarged photo of the suspect piece of paper.

"That was our day."

"A question not asked is truth unfound" announced Bible. "Does anyone have any questions and comments on the first day of what might be termed the "Street Cleaner" murder?
.
Questions followed with Amy and Kalum, each taking turns to answer:

"Do you think the homeless man might be involved?" No

"What did the shooter retrieve from the ground?" Presumably the spent cartridge cases

"If this street Cleaner case is number 2, could the Sparrow Green case be number one?" Possible, though the method of murder was different.

"Do you think the killer has a list?" Well, he may but we have no evidence of a list.

"Is the killer a vigilante? "Maybe, given the words he was heard to say to the deceased.

"Did the dead dog have a name tag"? "No chorused Aerial and Johnathan to together". The questions earning "you're a time waster" look for Bible and a few low chuckles from members of the assembled group.

After a while the questions and suggestions subsided.

Bible announced the briefing on the "Sparrow" Green case.

Amy tried hard to follow the progress in the Sparrow Green case which was composed of interview of known associates of Green that canvassed enemies, those with grudges, possible vendettas etc. but no real progress.

Amy listened for a while but again her family switched into her head. From time to time, she jerked herself back to reality. The Sparrow Green Case did not carry the same markings as the Harrison case.

Death followed a stabbing. No witnesses, so no one heard any arguments, comments or shouting. Forensics had only turned up a shoe print of size 12 of some worn shoes, which you could buy at a discount department store. The killer drove away in a late model white Hi Ace which a passer-by a street over noticed as the vehicle had no plates. No DNA no fingerprints well at least anything that was on record, no discarded clothing. Interviews to date had not turned up anything new.

Street Cleaner

The usual non-committal statement has gone out to the press. "We are pursuing a number of lines of investigation." Still Green and Harrison were considered by their "colleagues" as part of Sydney's Criminal intelligentsia, so a tie in is possible.

16. Another witness, "another story"

The (1800) six o'clock meeting had not revealed anything
new for Amy or Kalum apart from the mysterious non
witness, Anosmia Smith bolting. Maybe he owed money and
was sneaking around trying to avoid detection. MR Smith was
possibly surprised when unexpectedly disturbed.

They had heard of the progress or really lack of progress on
the Sparrow Green case. Could both cases be linked? The
meeting at least got everyone up to speed with both active
cases.

Another meeting awaited Amy and alum. They arrived for
their meeting with Waleed Taha. The manager at the bar had
proved to be very helpful. He had contacted some other bar
and hotel owners in the area leaving a message that if they
saw Taha that he was not in trouble, but the police wanted to
talk to him about anything he saw the night before, the night
of the murder.

The message had got through to Taha who had rung in and
asked the bar manager what it was about and when the
police would be by. The manager arranged a meeting for
12:30PM and reassured Taha it had nothing to do with him, it
only concerned what he had seen. They are interviewing
witnesses about what they saw.

"He still has some doubts" added Geoff the manger. His
escape from ROSS (Republic of Southern Sudan) has led him
to be suspicious of everyone not least of all the police. He
said he would be able to arrange his work to be here around

the arranged time. He is an excellent cleaner, but I doubt that I would see him more often than once every few months. His work tells me he has been here"

Amy and Kalum sat down to wait. Both declined an alcoholic drink but accepted a coffee, a not unusual offering by some bars trying to cater to a wider audience. When it arrived, it was clear to both of them that it was made from a quality bean. Not the instant that was found back at the office.

Part way through their coffees a man walked in and looked around. The man was tall and had skin colouration of a Sudanese. He looked fit with eyes that were bright His clothing was a pair of overalls with Taha Cleaning services on the upper left-hand side of the overalls where you might find a pocket. He wore safety boots that met safety standards but were not thick and heavy. He carried a backpack vacuum cleaner and sundry cleaning items in a bucket. This was the man. To confirm it he walked up to Amy and Kalum and introduced himself as Waleed Taha.

Kalum led off. "Thanks for coming into see us. I know you are busy. I am Acting Detective Sergeant Kalum Menzies and with me is Acting Detective Inspector Amy Whitelaw. We are investigating…: Waleed broke in "the James Harrison shooting." "That's right" confirmed Amy. "I understand that you were on the premises at the time of the shooting, can confirm that and tell us what you saw?

"Indeed, I was here, working", Waleed confirmed. It was apparent to Amy; from the way he spoke that this man was better educated than most cleaners Amy had met.

Street Cleaner

"I was mopping the floor and had taken the dirty water out onto the street, to flush it down the drain. I looked down the street and saw two men in conversation. The voices became louder as I was emptying out the water. I was too far away to tell what they were saying. As I stood up from emptying the bucket, another man walked past me headed in the direction of the men in discussion. He had passed me before I could see his face. I had no reason to take note of his features. I thought nothing of it and continued to rinse out my mop, when I heard a car leaving quickly. One of the two men in the street had left. The man who had passed me was now in conversation with the remaining man, then the first shot, followed by a second shot. The shooter bent down and seemed to pick something up and discarded what looked like a piece of paper, which floated in the air, there was a slight breeze and then fell on the road. He, the shooter continued onto towards George Street, rounded the corner and disappeared"

Amy followed up with a question, "So after the shooter left the scene what did you do"?

"I retreated into the bar doorway but watching, as I was concerned that I could become a target as he walked away.

"What about helping the man who was shot, your fellow human being?" asked Kalum with slight negativity evident in his voice

"My old country is one that is now filled with rage and war. The Republic of Southern Sudan started out as a homeland for the Sudanese people, separate from the Arab people in the north. However, the peace of the new country was short lived. The country is now involved in a bloody civil war. You don't see anything in Sudan if you want to stay alive. You certainly don't get involved.

I was fortunate to come to Australia and get my little business going. I told you what I saw. However, I cannot afford to get involved. Getting involved may backfire on me. I am here in Australia legally, but I am still not a citizen. I told you what I saw."

Amy and Kalum listened to an explanation not unknown among immigrants living in Australia. Though many people that arrived seeking a peaceful life felt unsure in their new country as they carried the concerns they had, had in their old countries with them into a new life. Waleed's story was not that unusual

Kalum spoke up. "You said the man came past you. Did you see anything distinctive about him, his walk his dress, any feature that may have been unusual or usual for that matter?"

What seemed an enduring silence followed, and it was apparent that Waleed, though not wanting to get involved was searching for something unique about the shooter.

A statement of facts broke the silence.

"His long black coat is something I have noticed some people wearing when I go past the law courts. The long coats are common in winter. What was different about this coat was that it had red under the collar, there was a red lining. His

Street Cleaner

collar was turned up as he passed but he turned it down once
he had passed.'

As he finished, Waleed held up his hand as if to require
silence. Amy waited and left any follow up that might be
needed to come from Kalum.

"As he turned his coat down, I noticed that his right hand had
what looked like a star on it. I could not see whether it was a
scar or a tattoo. The star appeared to be rough in shape. It
looked uneven, but it was dark, and I only had a brief view in
the light from the bar."

It was now early morning. It was clear Waleed had told them
all he knew or at least, what came to him that he knew.
Thanking him for his time and turning to leave Waleed felt
the need to repeat what he had said earlier.

"I told you what I saw."

A final reinforcement of his truthfulness and his apparent
lack of trust in authority he had brought with him to Australia

Part 3 - Another murder? - To not solve one murder maybe careless but now we have three

17. Ivan Stromboli – Number 3

The meeting with Waleed Taha had taken the case into its second twenty-four hours. As Amy got into her car, she recounted the days' events in her mind. The witnesses to the shooting the nature of the kill and the mysterious number 2 She recalled the interviews through-out the day. Put it aside she told he mind

It was essential she had some sleep and be back into work by 0800.

Sleep of a sort came quickly but the case occupied her dreams. No fulsome sleep tonight. The thought of the odd so called homeless man and his identification of the arguing parties. The two female attaches and what they saw floated into view. The bar cleaner and his story and the non-story of Eli Korobiete entered her dream/ No fluffy white clouds just a host of witnesses. The deceased man alive again telling her he knew who shot him but disappearing before he could make the final statement

Sleep drifted on and the dreams eventually drifted away as the early morning came. Pleasant thoughts filled her sleep, her time as a child, her parents, and her brother when they were all holidaying at the beach down the coast. Thoughts of happier times more innocent times broken by the sound of her mobile, intruding on a childhood adventure. Sleepily she looked at her phone with the number showing that Bible's office number had disturbed her.

"Hi Bible, we have met with the Bar cleaner, up late, why the call so early", noticing he mobile showed 5:21 am.

"I bring you bad tidings, another murder and we may have a serial murderer or murderers on our hands. You need to get down to Broadway"

Another death! This was not good news at the start of day two of the investigation. Kalum had been rung as well but had slept through the ring of his phone. He texted Amy before she left home that he would meet her on Broadway in a little over an hour. Amy began the forty-to-fifty-minute drive. She asked herself, why does this killer strike at night? Could he not be more thoughtful and kill during business hours or at least after seven?

The trip to Broadway, which is a seven hundred metre strip of road that separated the suburbs of Ultimo and Chippendale, was uneventful. The street formerly known as George Street South and then as George Street West become The Broadway, which was shortened in the tradition of truncating names in Australia to just Broadway. Amy, with siren screaming ignored some of the restrictions imposed on George Street after the advent of the trams and made the drive in far less time than normal

Broadway extended beyond a road name to be recognised at least by those people who frequented it to be the name of the area the street passed through. Once an important area for trading and commerce, which housed a major department store now gone, a brewery now gone, a variety of hotels, drinking houses rather than a place to stay, three universities and a TAFE college, with the department store site and closed brewery now redeveloped into shopping eating locating and high density, impressive expensive housing.

As Amy pulled up to the barrier which blocked traffic from entering the crime scene some early morning commuters had become a gawking crowd. The early morning peak hour was almost upon the scene with the streets nominated as detours starting to become clogged. There were detours for cars coming from the west heading to the south and as far north as the light rail permitted. Traffic was banking up and questions were being asked of patrolling police of how one would get to certain parts of the city, given the street linking to parts of the city was blocked.

Police were working further along Broadway directing drivers to turn off the road when the drivers wanted to go straight ahead.

Blocked city streets had become the norm in Sydney for some time following the commencement of the operation the light rail and efforts to turn Sydney from being car centred to a pedestrian oasis. The much-vaunted light rail had seen George Street now permanently closed to traffic from the start of the service. Years had gone by with George street being dug up and re dug, resulting in a few pedestrians, being the only form of travelling life to navigate the closed off streets, which they now shared with trams. Small businesses had seen their trade decline, during the building works and in some cases dwindle to the point where closure was the only way to stop losing money.

There was no Plan B in transport planning to cope with a murder causing blockage of streets and traffic chaos on a street that usually allowed entry from the outer areas to the city centre and one of the main paths of escape to the west.

Amy parked her car next to the outer barrier and sorted out who was the police officer in charge of the crime scene. A woman of approximately fifty years of age identified herself as the officer in charge.

Senior Sergeant Karen Williams had an authoritative style in the way she held herself and how she presented as overseeing the situation. She and Amy exchanged greetings in a professional, though not in a warm way. No unexpected given the scene that faced them. Karen Williams outlined what was known to Amy.

"000 got call at 4:42 that there was a man lying on the road. A motorist had spotted the deceased as he approached the body in his car. He initially assumed the person was drunk and contacted the police. I and to two of my other officers attended the scene, which we began cordoning off with our two cars and erecting tape, once we had ascertained the person was apparently deceased. The ambulance, which was rung by 000, arrived approximately two minutes after us and confirmed the man was deceased. Preliminary analysis is that there are two gunshot wounds to the head.

In relation to management of the scene I rang back to the station and asked for more people for traffic control and then contacted forensics who got here about fifteen minutes before you. The council has an all-night number, and I rang them to get some wooden barriers down here. They arrived after the ambulance left. I want to assure you that the scene has been secured since we arrived and no one apart from the gloved ambulance officers and forensics team have been near the body or inside the perimeter." Karen concluded her precise and concise summary

The she turned her report to the victim. "There are no identification documents we could see without disturbing the body but I can tell you the deceased is Ivan Stromboli. A large amount of cash was found on the body, some of the notes had fallen from the pocket of his coat. We removed the rest with gloves on as some were starting to blow away. When counted turned out to be $6,000. Something must have occurred for someone even like Stromboli to have than much on his person

Anything you need. I and my two officers who were with me at the first response are happy to help." Karen identified a young woman who was policing one edge of the scene and a young man policing the other side of the perimeter." Amy noted that both held the rank of Senior Constable and to Amy both were well in charge of the scene with their quickly evident quiet and authoritative manner

.

"Any witnesses?" asked Amy. "One driver and a few people who were walking past on the other side of the road. We have their names, mobile number, addresses etc. Though we have not found anyone yet who was close to what happened". Came back the reply.

Amy noted the scene was under control. Karen and her team, now of three had it well and truly under control. Outside the crime scene there were traffic police who were moving people on even though some people began to challenge them as they got agitated by the delays and detours.

Street Cleaner

A newly arrived officer worked in the same effective way as the other two with Karen overseeing the scene. All four experienced and disciplined officers. These initial responders were well and truly in charge of the crime scene. All were quiet but authoritative in their presence and the words spoken to anyone who managed to get by the external traffic police were quiet but concise and authoritative. Amy felt sure that nothing had been touched since their arrival at the scene.

Amy went over to view the body. Even standing some distance from the body it was clear to her that it was Ivan Stromboli. Stromboli was an inner-city crime figure, more interested in fencing stolen items than being directly involved in crime. He had been charged several times with being in possession of stolen goods but had been able to walk away when each time he was arrested. Someone would come forward to say they had left the goods on the property of Stromboli without permission or his knowledge.

The second local crime figure to die in two days and the third in a month. It was looking as Bible had stated that this might be the actions of a serial murderer. It could not be a coincidence that three crime figures had died in such a short time. Just as she was about to talk to the forensic team about anything they may have found so far, Senior Sergeant Karen Williams touched Amy's arm.

"We have a member of the public identify a poster on a window as possibly having something to do with the death. It is over in the window where the young blonde-haired woman is standing."

Amy headed in the direction of the young woman. "How did you see this?" Amy asked the young woman as she walked up to her." "I stopped to check my hair is ok in the window before I went into work. I work (and study) at the college three doors down."

Amy was listening but the words slid away as she read the typed note in the window. The witness slipped away as Amy looked back to the scene and again at the notice.

When will you people learn? I am cleaning the streets of those people who are criminals but are either not caught or caught and not duly punished. This is number - 3.

1. *Sparrow Green*

2. *James Harrison*

3. *Ivan   Stromboli*

There will be more unless the legal system or someone stops these types of people getting away with the crimes they commit. Bible had been right we do have a serial killer with a mission, on our hands

As Amy stood rereading the note taking it in a whisk of blonde hair had now disappeared up the street. Later investigation would reveal the woman had been paid by a delivery agency to paste up the note and make sure the police noticed it. The agency usually dealt with parcel delivery but there had been a walk in, to their office. He paid cash. a lot of cash, for the delivery and display of the notice, which when delivered to the dispatch desk was in a sealed envelope. The envelope was to be opened when the delivery person arrived at the scene. The job was tagged to a man named Solomon. The woman had only opened the envelope as directed at the scene and pasted up the notice.

Cameras at the agency showed what appeared to be a man, in a hoodie which covered his face. Gloves covered his hands.

Nothing to see.

18. 'Why didn't they grasp it earlier?"'

It was an early start for the Cleaner who watched the news box at the bottom of his television screen. No real news as yet. A Sea Lion had to be removed from a wharf where it had taken up residence. Still no details of the 'kill' apart from breaking news of a death on Broadway. Details to follow.

Questions ran through the mind of the Cleaner

- Does the important work I am doing need an email and a tweet to explain it?

- Is social media the only way to communicate? Can't people read from my actions what I am trying to achieve?

- Why didn't they know what was happening from day one?

He spoke to the audiences of one, himself. "These odd job organisations provide a ready supply of causal labour for any task. Surely paying the delivery service to put up the poster and let the police know it was there, enabled the police to get the message.

The next communication will need to be more extensive. Blogger, Patrick Silver the best source for breaking news in the city, should be informed of future plans."

Street Cleaner

The Cleaner was exasperated with the efforts of police not being able to work out what was being accomplished. "Surely Acting Inspector Amy Whitelaw and her offsider Kalum Menzies have worked out what I am trying to achieve." he said for his own benefit.

Comfortable now with a red wine, his drink of choice propped up in bed, the Cleaner was sure the police had found and understood the message. Although there was no talk of it on ay news source at the moment.

Thoughts ran through his mind. "I know the judiciary will never change. Political correctness and full gaols will lead to more of those criminals in charge of the organised crimes of our city not being caught, or even if caught and then convicted earning a punishment with little more than token gaol time, community service or what appears to be a large fine but in relative terms is an inconsequential cost of doing business.

What should I do to make it clear to the criminal classes that when you escape the courts you cannot escape me?

I must be careful. I have been only minutes from being caught.

Today was my most public corrective action. Can I afford to be so public in future? Should I worry about being seen or caught? The cleaning of the streets is a commitment I have made to myself. No one but me has any responsibility to set things right."

Street Cleaner

Sleep started to descend on the Cleaner like a gentle curtain, blocking the brain from further thinking.

19. Johnathan and Aerial take charge

The blond hair stuck out from under the fedora hat. The witness who called herself Caroline, which was proved to be her name, as the license she produced verified with a picture that was far from flattering.

Initially her dress and demeanour created speculation by Johnathan and Aerial as they viewed her along with an accompanying man as to whether that was a working name. Her clothes appeared to be mismatched or at least of contrasting colours, a purple shirt, and a gold skirt. A long black beaded necklace falling to her waist with black track shoes. But a ready explanation for her dress became clear.

Caroline had a clasp purse with her, the sort the British Royal family carried to avoid having to shake hands with any crowd member's hand they did not wish to shake. However no all royals were reluctant to shake hands. The latest woman to marry into the Royal family was known for her willingness to shake hands and even to hug crowd members. Her previous successful television acting career seemed have been a great apprenticeship for her married life, though it turned out no top be so

Apollo an "Olympic God,"…..not in this case, a short but somewhat well-built man who wore a now crumpled suit and apologised for his appearance in that he said his clothes had been fresh from cleaning the previous day when he and Caroline had ventured out. Apollo was somewhat better colour coordinated though than Caroline. Aerial had suggested to Johnathan, his blue shirt, and dark suit, and black track shoes appeared coordinated. However, he explained the night had proved long and exciting, leading to his somewhat dishevelled appearance. There was no need at this stage to ask what source of the excitement of the previous evening had been. Apollo carried what proved to be uniforms for a large supermarket shop which turned out two branded shirts, branded with the brand of one of the leading supermarket chains and two black pairs of trousers.

Caroline and Apollo had arrived in the early morning of the murder at "murder central" as named by the media. Johnathan had been on his way in when he got the call about the need to interview two witnesses. He called Aerial who had also received a call and was on her way and just a few minutes behind Johnathan in arriving. Earlier they had received the call about the Stromboli murder and without being told they knew they would be needed to do background on Ivan Stromboli's, known associates, enemies, possible connection to the previous murders and some of the witness interviews.

The four who were in a police interview room sitting opposite each other, looking for a moment like two couples who were here for a breakfast meeting. Johnathan leading off, 'So you told the desk sergeant that you witnessed the murder?"

Caroline answered, saying that it was her idea to come in but that she was not sure how much they had seen would be helpful to the police

"Caroline why don't you start off", continued Johnathan.

"We had been out for the night and were on our way back to my place when we saw a man walk quickly past us. I did not take much notice till I saw what I thought was a gun come out of his pocket just after he passed us. I motioned to Apollo who put his finger to his lips which Caroline demonstrated in an overt manner as if sharing the signal with a child who may not have seen it before. Apollo nodded agreement, a silent confirmation.

"I can't tell you about the gun, I don't know anything about guns. He held the gun low against is leg, pointing it towards the ground sort of hiding it in his coat. The gun seemed to disappear into the folds of his coat once he lowered it.

Any way he walked on and approached two men. They were talking to each other and seemed to be doing some sort of deal though it was hard to hear what they were saying as they were talking as if they didn't want anyone to hear.

Apollo, broke in, "though I did hear the words – 'that is not enough for the package', when one of them raised his voice. The man, who passed over the money, dipped into his pocket and appeared to come out with more notes"

Caroline nodded agreement and then carried on. She was either the dominant member of the two or they agreed she could do most of the talking.

"Once the man passed, we watched him go further up the street while standing in some shadows. There was the exchange of words between the two men. The man who was shot looked like he got the money while the other man got a package. As they parted the man who received the package must have said something funny as they smiled and shook hands. As the man with the package moved away, he turned towards the approaching shooter, though the man with the box didn't appear to recognise him. The man with the money turned back and must have noticed the gun and yelled to the other man that the approaching man was "a shooter"; well that is what he said. Both men were now trying to run away from the shooter, but too late as the shooter raised his gun and fired. The shot man fell and started to try to get up, but the man with the gun shot him again in the head. The other man had now disappeared around a corner into the next street."

"So what did you do, did you check whether the man who was shot was dead?" asked Aerial.

"We were frozen for a moment and then backed away. I pulled Caroline away and we headed back the way we came till we came to a coffee shop where we stayed and discussed what to do over a coffee breakfast', chimed in Apollo.

"Then we decided" at which point Caroline had broken in over Apollo "that we should come back here. We had seen a shooting and should report what we know. So here we are?

Aerial continued "Why were you still out at that time in the morning?"

Apollo explained that he and Caroline worked as pickers, "they call us personal shoppers, but we work in a warehouse picking, filling online customer orders in a "dark store" for a supermarket chain. We decided to go out after we finished work at around 12:30 AM. We weren't working tomorrow, I mean today.

Though, the city is dead these days we decided to try this part of the city for a late dinner and drinks. We got into a place further west just after 1:00, ate till around three and then we decided to head home and get some sleep. We walked slowly and decided to get some coffee at a café. We had come from a café that opens early for breakfast. Caroline lives in George Street in a hotel, a pub, not the ritzy type of place. We are looking for a flat. I moved from the country to take the job and met Caroline at work."

"So what did the shooter look like?" asked a patient Aerial.

"Tall, wearing a long black coat, work boots, you known the boots people wear in factories or road workers."

"Anything else, physical features, anything about the coat", asked Johnathan.

Apollo looked at Caroline and then replied "We did not see his face. His hair was dark and there was nothing unusual about his coat, which is the only clothes we saw, but there was a hint of red protruding below the collar of the coat" Caroline checked with Apollo who shrugged his shoulders and concluded, "nothing else, though you said he had something on his hand." Yes that's true responded Caroline but I could not tell what I was."

"I know you have been up for some time, but we need to get your statement down in writing," stated Aerial while signalling to a uniformed officer who received instructions to take the formal statements, give them coffee, together.

"Together?" inquired Jonathan a she Aerial left the interview room.

"I am not sure there is much more they can give us, and they clearly have pieced their story together as a couple, but we can still talk to them individually if we turn up something contradictory."

20. Another day, another dawn, another kill...?

A few days on from the third kill, well technically number five, counting the two in New Zealand it was another day, another dawn, another awakening, for The Cleaner this time with a relatively clear mind.

He awoke not wanting to miss his chance. It was just a few days from when he first returned to action as a bringer of justice or was, he a monster. His mind sparked between the two extremes. The press had published fanciful stories of his venture. Creating several possible scenarios to explain the killing of his victim. Revenge for past sins. Another gang wiping out an opposition head. A past victim of the criminal taking revenge.

Today would be another justice problem solved. Justice would be done, not just seen to be done as is the case in the hands of the courts.

He knew the intended target would be late in the day travelling to a charity ball. The future victim was out of the game at the moment having lost momentum in his "business dealings" while inside prison. The target on early release was required to not meet with his past colleagues, which meant security would be minimal at his house given his past security had been current or ex "crims". None of his old associates had been visible since his release. Security would be, or at least should be light, given it was provided by a local security firm.

Street Cleaner

His house where he lived with his wife was three stories in part, but in the main it was two complete stories. There was a third story over the main bedroom. Speculation was that that the third story was a watching post as you could see traffic in the street as well as the front and back yards. Speculation was such that before he went to prison a watcher with a high-powered rifle, possibly one used by snipers was positioned day and night in the upper level. Fake news said today's future victim to media suggestions of a guard house on the roof. Certainly, today the top level window appeared to be closed and curtained. No one was visible.

The self-appointed avenger, judge of justice, planned to lure his new victim out of the house. It had to be here, he reassured himself without speaking. The ball posed too many problems. The city, the people, and the security around the ball, worked against his success.

His plan centred on using the bush area at the back of the victim's property to his advantage. A fire was likely to draw attention. The bush was wet from the rain of several nights ago. He brought an accelerant with him. Just petrol. No need for anything more exotic.

Surprisingly, he felt more settled about his actions than he expected. Maybe this justice crusade would provide him with a kind of peace which would stand him well once it was completed, a contribution to society, though there was no way for the Cleaner to tell when the end of the killing spree would come.

Street Cleaner

The house of the next victim was in an outer suburb of Sydney. The street had many substantial houses, some owned by questionable people, well at least so the media said.

The occupants of the victim's house felt close to their roots, close to their family. They lived in an area where the two adults, man and wife that owned the large house, had grown up. They never wanted to be in the city. They had decided to live away from the location where their work often occurred. Even so, they planned to stay in the city tonight. This would allow them to enjoy the ball with a short trip to bed.

It was to be here and now at the family house. The killer walked approximately two kilometres from where he had left his car and was now positioned in the bush adjoining the victim's yard, close enough to see the back of house. At the back of the house was an everyday security guard wearing a uniform of a locally owned security outfit. Our killer knew that another guard wearing the same uniform was at the front of the house. The intended victim was inside the house. The intended victim's favourite day car, yes there was also a night car, was in the front driveway. Our so-called justice avenger had seen the day car drive by when circling through the bush, gleaming duco, evidence of a recent wash.

Now standing in the driveway, gleaming in the sun surrounded by a small film of water following its daily wash, stood the day car. The intended victim never went anywhere during the day without his car. The media claimed it was his pride and joy and claimed to quote him as saying that it was the only car for him during the day. Tangible evidence for all to see of his success.

Street Cleaner

The car was a 1958 Dodge Custom Royal that had been lovingly restored to show room condition. Fully rebuilt. Push button auto and still running the 350 Wedge engine. The car had been top of the Dodge models during its production from 1955 through to 1958 and presented as showroom black in colour. The Cleaner laughed silently to himself that the colour, though generally standard with this model of car, may represent its owner's character and conscience.

A newspaper, some kindling soaked in petrol along with a few branches from a dead tree he had collected along the way that had escaped the rain were the starting point for a fire. Smoke would rise from other wood, which was still wet, as the fire caught hold. The fire was lit and burning.

No movement from the guard. Half asleep, sitting, enjoying the sun? A noise was required to gain the attention of the apparently disinterested guard before the fire burnt out in the wet surrounds. But what noise. Fortunately, the noise of a loud revving of car turning into the street and passing the house on the street side jolted the guard though in the backyard awake. He looked up, and after focusing for a few seconds yelled, "Fire." The guard banged on the back door, yelling fire several times. In a few seconds the intended target was in the yard setting up a hose, while he commented that it looked small, probably a cigarette discarded by a neighbour who smoked in the bush.

The intended victim dragged the hose closer to our killer. The avenger was concealed in the bush. If the soon to be victim knew his killer was positioned off to his right, he would likely have seen him. If you can see your prey than they are likely to be able to see you.

Carefully the Cleaner moved forward. The now awake backyard guard had been joined by the front yard guard who were both beating some of the burning bush with straw brooms they had picked up. Several other people had left the house and were now rushing with buckets to the fire location.

Though the brooms were the only firefighting appliance the guards found at hand, the owner had now hooked up and armed himself, with the hose which he pointed towards what appeared to be the centre of the fire. Closer the killer crept, with the owner fully occupied with the smoking emergency.

Suddenly the owner turned and saw the killer, but his gaze was disrupted by calls from the house next door with a neighbour hanging over the fence giving instructions. "It is more to your right." The killer thought of how thankful he was of neighbours with useless advice.

The killer took a chance, stepping forward, but with the hood of the hoodie he wore pulled down covering most of his face. Two silenced shots put the victim on the ground. Several people in the yard saw the killer emerge from the bush and the home owner fall, but they seemed frozen in time. Shock at what was occurring.

There was a quick withdrawal by the neighbour from over the fence who had provided a final, fatal distraction. No one went immediately to the aid of the victim as the killer shot the now fallen victim in the chest and in the head.

Then the killer walked away with increasing speed while seemingly everyone else at least temporarily seemed to be frozen in time. Each person seemed to be without consciousness apparently trying to place the shooting event into a schema which they understood. A fire then a shooting, was it too much for the watching throng.

However, the pause was short, followed by screaming and yelling of those the killer left behind trying to fight the fire and help the victim. Seconds went by stretching into minutes till calls to an emergency number were made for help, while at the same time trying to assist the man on the ground, who was dead after the shot to the head. Confusion on what to do first. The only person who would have been able to take charge of a scene such as this was now dead.

Making quick time back to his car, knowing he had a short period to leave the scene he worked on moving his car. The killer, driving the car to comply with local traffic speed requirements saw a local garbage truck came into view. "Garbage day, great". Turning a corner and getting ahead of the truck he stopped and deposited the gun and the unused bullets, which he had wiped down, into a bin in time for the approaching garbage truck to scoop it up with the rest of detritus. Sirens were approaching and then they had gone past.

Ditch the hoody in a waste burning bin he knew of at a local service station, with no one seeing him as he made his way out of the area. Turning the two-way garment inside out so the brown lining became the garment's exterior as it burned. No speed cameras and no private security cameras on the roads he took. He had checked for cameras and though sweating profusely he knew he had got away.

21. Some specialist help from Doctor Davina

Aerial went off to see if the coroner had some early information on what at the moment was the latest murder while Johnathan was waiting for Amy sitting in her visitors chair in her office, which Bible had rescued from being a storeroom, at least for the time she was on this investigation.

When Amy came in and without a hello, Johnathan charged right in, "There is a person who I knew in Canberra who is in Sydney for a conference who thinks she has some ideas on the profile of the Cleaner "

"And good morning to you Johnathan," smiled Amy through tired eyes as she took off her coat hung it over her chair. No hanging hooks in converted storerooms. "Have you had coffee?" enquired Amy

"Not yet I was waiting to brief you on the witness report", Johnathan replied as Amy produced a coffee for her and one for him. I knew someone would want one. I bought two. No one should drink alone." Aerial entered the offie sthey both took their first sip.

Amy listened attentively to the report on Aerial's and Johnathan's encounter with Apollo and Caroline.

"Well I know one more thing though it is not likely to be important, our killer wears work boots", Amy responded.

.

Johnathan hit on a pause to put forward his idea. "We have had an offer from a Doctor Davina Gillespie to provide us with her insights. She is", Johnathan paused "a behavioural theorist, professor at Australian National University (ANU), and hence a profiler for the AFP in Canberra. She did great work on several of the few murders the AFP had to solve. She is the one I was going to suggest earlier we should contact.

What is she doing in Sydney?" chimed in Amy

" Apparently she is up here speaking at and attending a conference on arousal theory, motivation and follow up behaviour at Western Sydney University (WSU), which apparently has nothing especially to do with the criminal class. She has a slot for us at 4:00 PM (1600) and will be here for all who could attend.

"Great lets have her. Johnathan, I know you are not the office boy but could you print up a brochure with her name and that she has information on our 'Cleaner' cases' and drop it around the various floors and email it out", jumped In Amy who was interested in the idea but wanted to get to other things

 "She may have useful profile information" stated Johnathan with some degree of anticipation

"I hope so, otherwise we will waste an hour sitting through a lecture that we could be using running down associates of the four as of yesterday now murdered" lamented Amy

As (4:00 PM) 16:00 was fast approaching a tall attractive woman with long dark hair and wearing a black almost full-length dress adorned with orange flowers probably Clivia's along the hem to about mid the lower leg perched on medium sized heels was being shown to Amy's office. As she introduced herself to Dr Davina a thought passed through Amy's mind that Johnathan knowing the good doctor could have been more than a professional interest.

But why should I be thinking of that. What does it have to do with me anyway?

Davina interrupted Amy's momentary thoughtful trance. "Amy is there a screen, or should I just show the slides on the wall?"

"No, no there is a screen. I will roll it down." With a quick press of a few buttons the screen concealed behind a half curtain on the fading squad room wall came down. Amy watched as the Dr booted up her computer while connecting to a data projector she had brought with her. It was clear that Dr Davina came prepared.

"One of the people working on this 'Cleaner' case, Johnathan Lewis Brown knows of your work", a statement that Amy wondered why she was making. Davina continued positioning her data projector on the screen and was all business for a good thirty seconds till she responded to Amy's spoken thoughts.

She slowly turned towards Amy. "Yes Johnathan and I worked as part of a team on several cases and in depth together on two cases in the past when he was with the AFP. Johnathan has a great mind for police work. He can put disjointed information together to paint a picture of possible events within the context of a case. In the cases we worked on, once we worked through a detailed profile and pieced together what was known about a case, Johnathan had arrested each of the culprits with two weeks of starting the investigations. In both of those cases, there was enough irrefutable evidence to convict each of them. The felons were seeking a deal before there was a chance to go to trial but the evidence got then the maximum. No deal with twenty years each "

Amy smiled a nervous smile, while Dr. Davina and turned back to setting up he presentation.

Fifteen people had arrived without either Amy or Dr Davina noticing. Most of the attending group at this stage were seated in the back row. It looked just like school. Another three, no in fact five more of the curious or possibly interested officers were coming towards the room. Johnathan and Aerial made up the last group of two.

It was time to start. Amy introduced the guest "My thanks to Dr. Davina Gillespie, a distinguished academic and a valuable source as a behavioural scientist to the Australian Federal Police, for giving up her time today. My thanks to all of you for attending today. Dr. Gillespie we look forward to what you have to tell us'

Polite applause, for Dr. Gillespie as Amy took a seat next to Aerial, with Johnathan and Kalum making up a foursome of the entire front row of attendees, although there were still six empty chairs. It was good, thought Amy to see that the team is keen even if others were not as interested enough to attend, though she rationalised everyone on the floor had pending cases they were working on.

"Thank you, Detective Whitelaw." Acting Inspector, please, thought Amy.

"Johnathan, it is nice to see you again." Johnathan smiled and nodded as Amy wiggled, and then she wondered about her reaction to the familiarity between Gillespie and Johnathan.

"Thank you everyone who is here for giving me your time today.

The profile you currently have of your murder is I believe accurate. It is as I understand d it:

Slide One

"The unsub, Unknown subject) is likely in their thirties or forties, with possible previous experience in killing people prior to this round of murders. We are all but sure it is a man, 1.8 to 2 metres tall who wears a black coat with a red trim, maybe a military coat, wears work boots and shoots with a 9 mm gun. He has a scar or tattoo on his right hand of an in determinant nature. He also has something against the justice system so we cannot rule out people who have been involved or who are currently involved in police, courts or the like.

It is more than likely a man, with (I would say) experience in the judicial system who is acting to remedy some perceived hole or laxity in the criminal system. Patience has run out and now he is righting wrongs as he sees them. His note gave evidence to this supposition that there is or has been some connection to the justice system.

As I understand it the information you have on the killer so far, is agreeing with my initial profile of a possible killer. I have studied the cases as they have occurred as much as is possible for an outsider and have undertaken some research into similar cases, in Australia and elsewhere. I have found a total of nineteen similar crimes across Australia, New Zealand that appear similar or similarly motivated to those committed here. For Australia and New Zealand it was a short search. As yet I have not contemplated a world-wide search but the data I have looked at allows me to make some prime facie assumptions.

A key finding from my research would indicate that it is likely that your, unsub, has killed before he started on his current killing spree. The lack of evidence found at each scene would speak to someone who has had previous experience or has been schooled by someone who has. The people being killed here are the criminals or accused criminals, who are unlikely to pass on tips to each other"

People shifted in their chairs, seemingly to focus their attention on Dr. Gillespie. The possibility of previous killing experience had been only touched on so far. Here was a proposition that it was part of the profile for The Cleaner.

Street Cleaner

Even the two detectives at the back of the room moved forward several rows, with new interest.

"In Australia I found a case from Western Australia."

A concise summary appeared on the screen.

> "You will note that in this case a small-time criminal had been charged with killing a person who owed another party money. The judge considered the prosecution case was not strong and purely circumstantial and allowed the career crim bail. While the crim was on bail he was murdered. No suspect was identified.
>
> An apparently disenfranchised (well at least in his mind) court official killed the judge in his driveway stabbing the judge to death. He believed that the judge allowing bail for the guilty man was typical of the lax way justice was served by some judges.
>
> "I conducted justice". His words in a letter the killer posted to the Attorney General. This contributed to his belief that the judge had let too many criminals 'slide through the system.' Again these are the words of the killer.
>
> In another case a court official in his confession upon being captured and charged, chronicled a series of decisions by the judge that he believed, were letting criminals escape justice. He was 36 years old, was a qualified solicitor, who had been working for a major law firm. In his own time, he carried out research on

major murder cases and was heard to say that he felt that some of the clients of the firm 'had got away with murder'. He left the firm and began working in prosecution for the courts. He was unable to achieve his version of justice. He resorted to violence. Evidence turned up after his conviction that pointed to him killing the bailed man.

It later transpired as part of his confession for killing of the judge he admitted to murdering one of the former firm, where he had worked clients. A case which had been unsolved till his confession.

One murder to achieve 'justice' led to a second. Two other similar murders have been under investigation but no evidence linking them to our former justice worker has been turned up. Yet another vigilante"

Not a new case to Amy or most people in the room. Some of the early interest began to peak and wane but everyone was still hanging in there.

"I found, sixteen cases and with more time I suspect I would have found a lot more. I did a quick overview of the United States. All perpetrators were aged from 33 to 37. All of them worked in the legal system in various capacities, court officer, legal researcher, paralegal, lawyer, and one was a lower court judge, who believed cases heard and referred onto the appropriate court were being bungled. The judge killed a high level judge and two defence lawyers. Over 10000 case appeared to fit the general criteria of your cases. To many to research

All of them killed both criminals they perceived had escaped a conviction because of legal decisions or murdered the judges and other legal officials they blamed for criminals getting away with it." Davina Gillespie used her fingers to act out speech marks.

"Based on my analysis I think your profile should include an age range of 32 to 38. There are many unsolved crimes in the U.S. so the age range may be biased in favour of the solved cases but based on what we do know it is the most likely age range.

Each of the people including in the Australian case had completed post school education to at least an Advanced Diploma or degree level, with the majority having a higher-level Graduate Certificate to a Masters' qualification though not always in law.

All of them were successful in their jobs and most had jobs that carried a medium level of responsibility, but more than half had taken leave from their jobs or had recently left their legal jobs.

None of those felons who left their jobs had taken a new job. All were unhappy with the justice system and told anyone who would listen about their unhappiness and their lack of confidence in people responsible for the day-to-day administration of the legal system. Too lax, favouring the crim, did not seek justice etc. were among the complaints registered with anyone who would listen.

Every one of them had, been involved with violent
death. Witnessed on a street, a relative, involved in a
car accident where someone was clearly culpable.

"So what did in find out about New Zealand?"

An apparently rhetorical question Davina asked herself,
shifting her presentation back closer to home.

"The first case was a stabbing of a small-time
criminal who had escaped prosecution because of a
ruling in his favour that there had been a break in the
chain of evidence, which the persecutor decided not
to appeal.

The second was a known drug dealer, who had been
jailed previously. This one was shot.

Investigations turned up an associate who wanted to
rise up the food chain quickly. Before any charges
were laid, someone else came forward and admitted
to the killings. The admission was ruled out as the
confessor was with a mate, who came forward and
stated the confessor was with him at the time of the
killing.

Apparently, the confessor admitted had wanted to
help his boss out. His boss, the associate of the
criminal who was killed had five people come
forward backed up by closed circuit television to say
he was with them. No developments since then.

Both of the 'executions/ killings' occurred two years ago. Then, there was nothing. No further action.

No arrests in either case have been made. All likely subjects have been questioned. I have put my theory to them two weeks ago that the killer may have been disillusioned with the legal system. The New Zealand police said they would consider my theory. I gained an impression that they were not highly motivated towards finding the killer and that they thought everyone was better off for the loss of the two crims

Only a blurred photograph side on of the killer calmly leaving the second crime scene from CCTV along the road a short time after the killing was all the indication that the killer existed. The photo gave enough information to give the approximate height of that killer and some information on his physique. It also showed that he wore a black coat as with the Sydney killings."

There was a stirring in the room as everyone moved forward in anticipation of more that might be revealed about the killer.

Over a short period of time Amy came alive and started to anger without saying a word. She thought to herself, "How come I don't know about these cases? I would have thought that New Zealand police would have followed up as the Cleaner case had featured on national news broadcasts." Amy was about to run from the room and phone her N.Z. contacts, when the good doctor went on.

"The first maybe a crime of opportunity, the second better planned. The bullet was recovered from the second killing. The suspect in New Zealand wore a black coat so as to hide his appearance. Not dissimilar from your suspect. Here is another New Zealand photograph."

A blurry photo appeared on the screen with little to show who the person was under a hat and the coat, except the clothing looked to be male and the person was tall.

"I think your killer could be the same perpetrator who killed in New Zealand. The gap between then and now possibly attributed to the suspect trying to get back on track and make the system work the way they believe it should. Then complete disillusionment and the new killing spree.

Aged somewhere from 35 to 38 he has likely worked in the legal system in some capacity for some time, now on leave or recently left. He may not have the time to work, research, pick his victims and kill.

I did not mention that more than 60% of those in the cases I researched were ex-military and/or what is termed reservists here. Several others were recreational shooters some without but most with prior or existing military involvement. The bullet in the New Zealand case came from a luger, 9 mm."

Leaving a moment for this to sink in, then she went on.

" You might add the possible exposure to guns in your profile.

I will pause for questions."

"What makes you think our killer is the same killer as in New Zealand"? Asked, Mowbray a detective with a distinguished police record who now past early retirement age, was now considering when the right time was for his retirement.

Davina Gillespie did not pause to think. This was a first up obvious question.

"Similarity of the crimes. The first one was a rush, spontaneous, the second prepared. Seemingly the same approach here as across the ditch."

A reference to the near nature of Australia and New Zealand and their long-time link with and to each other, though Amy was beginning to feel they were not as close as countries as she would have thought.

"It is the same pattern. The killer tries to make it work when they return to Australia but eventually falls into the same pattern."

Amy chipped in announcing that Dr. Gillespie must leave but get in a question "Did they test the bullet?"

"Yes Amy. But there was no match to your crimes. The bullet showed the gun barrel was not standard. I am sure they can send you a report."

Then the room was empty apart from Amy and her team.

After thanking and showing the Doctor out, Amy took the moment to speak in a way to lift the team. Well at least she thought she was lifting the team. 'We are only a few days into the investigation. We have only just linked the first murder to the others and just now heard of how some New Zealand murders may be linked to our investigation, which needs to be followed up today. Kalum could you get onto the New Zealand police and while you are sourcing their files, you might ask them why they did not contact us earlier."

Kalum nodded enthusiastically when he knew he could have a lash at another police force about their apparent tardiness.

Amy went on. However, I think we should widen our investigation and look at the murders from a different perspective. In the arrest of Ivan Malat, (a convicted serial killer, whose case was known to all of the team, who preyed on hitch hikers south of Sydney) the approach, most often taken, and we have taken, of starting at the crime scene was reversed by a single officer who looked at the crime families that had ready access to the highway to the Belanglo state forest (where Malat attacked, raped some victims and burnt their bodies while taking what he deemed valuables from their possessions).

"I am suggesting" went on Amy "in this case we might start with people working in the legal system in the greater Sydney area, for unhappy employees, who may be currently working or are possibly on leave who often complain about the absence of punishment for criminals as well as how the system lets them go. In investigating existing staff, we might also turn up other people who have left in the last year that expressed their dissatisfaction on how the system had failed. Johnathan and Aerial, you start on a hit list, and start accessing it, local courts, legal aid, yes, I know that may not seem a logical choice but we need not to discount anyone working in the law, Attorney General's Department etc.

Johnathan and Aerial seemed to be positively delighted to be talking to someone else apart from the local criminal intelligentsia (or lack of it.)

Amy thought about the Belanglo strategy, which came to her not as a thought-out approach but more as a reflex action while listening to Dr. Gillespie. Thinking of crime families that had everyday access to the forest had turned up a suspect family in short time. Would the legal workforce do the same in this case?

Would sort of thinking would help in this case(s)? It was still early.

Yes, the killings were adding up but wasn't it still early? Something new had been revealed about the cases. How could this new information help the investigation? Why had New Zealand not made contact?

22. "Now we are guarding 'the crooks",

Kalum read from the email that had just arrived in his inbox.

"We have a new directive saying everything should be done to ensure any prominent criminal figures are advised that there may be a threat to their life. We are to warn them of a possible threat to their lives and ask if they would like advice on how they can protect themselves. In some cases, protection should be offered to these people where staff can be spared.

Protection may include:

'1. Suggestions on likely security firms that could provide patrol services around where they are living or staying or,

2. A police presence if there is a perceived threat to any individual or the family of an induvial who has been threatened or is a credible current or potential threat."

"So now we are protecting the felons", ranted Kalum to no one in particular. Kalum was not known for having a temper, at least one that led to shouting. Several heads had turned at the noise but there was no initial disagreement with his response to the new directive.

Amy sitting close-by was in the mood to agree with Kalum but restrained herself. None of the victims would be missed by anyone. One mother had said she regretted the day she had given birth to her now deceased criminal son. However, Amy felt the need to try to justify the directive. It needed some spin to make it seem as though it was an acceptable request. Everyone had by now looked up after hearing the outburst from Kalum

Amy surveyed the room and began her rationale for the legitimacy of the directive "What happens if someone not involved gets killed? What if a bystander who has nothing to do with the crim or in any of our cases is injured or killed. If we are not ensuring some of the likely targets are protected then the likelihood of someone not involved, the innocent, being hurt is increased?"

Amy felt any response that she was to give was not being genuine. However, she was the boss and had to hold the departmental line, Kalum she knew was right though for different reasons. The need to divert officers from other cases or divert officers from investigation of the current "Cleaner" cases would slow up all current investigations and make further killings more likely.

Amy tried "It is just as important to prevent crimes as it is to investigate them."

Kalum ranted on "But all the murders have been targeted, even the first one. No one from the public has been close enough to any of the killings to be involved let alone be injured or worse. As they say "We need a bigger boat", a reference to movie where a people eating shark that was trolling the waterways near a small beach side town, who many of the people living in the town including the council wanted to ignore because of the impact on the summer trade. In this case we need a bigger team"

Street Cleaner

Exactly what I think. Kalum is right, though I can't be seen to be agreeing. I must stay positive. I must keep everyone else positive and focussed on the key game, catching the Cleaner, and soon.

I hope tomorrow is a rostered day off for the 'Cleaner'.

We need to make some progress, though it is still only early in the investigation.

Part 4 – No one dies today "what a shame"

23. Where it all began for the Cleaner

"I wish this had never started." the Cleaner said to himself in almost a whisper. He ran through the sequence of events that brought him too today.

"I am always reliving the kills I made on the New Zealand holiday that started my killing spree. The thoughts of anguish during the two-year gap between New Zealand and now where I tried with counselling and prescribed drugs to overcome my thoughts. The spree beginning again that was not yet over and may never be over, becomes as real again to me as If was murdering my recent victims over and over again..

I started with an opportunistic situation where information supplied allowed me to follow my target to where he would be. I have been confronted with men who in my mind turned into my prey.

A moment of recognition appeared in the eyes of several, of my victims. I knew the soon to be dead criminal thought he or she recognised my face, a face he clearly recalled from an earlier meeting in different surroundings. Such recognition called for swift action.

The knife I carried, in my first murder as an avenger of justice, which was for my personal protection, appeared in my hand and plunged itself into the stomach of my first opponent and then drove upward towards the heart. Though

Street Cleaner

I held the knife it seemed to have a will and a purpose of its own.

Why did I always carry the knife? Was it for protection, revenge or did I just invent a sense of self concern to validate my mission? Why did I always have the knife even though I shot some of my prey? What was and is my mission, revenge, justice, or the exercise of power?

Why really did I want to strike down these people? Was it fear of what might happen if I did not strike or, did I strike because the opportunity was there? Was it rage that drove me or was it, fear of what they might do in the future? My fear was a fear for society.

Why on the first time I killed in New Zealand was my prey out without protection? Where had been his protective group of associates? Would I have paused if there had been others around? Was this just a time given to me to exercise my will outside of failing justice systems? What if his attack had gone badly would I have continued?

The news reports that followed my first kill were that the victim had wanted to walk alone in the early morn. The press statements made by his "group of associates" suggested some of them wanted go with him, but he needed some alone time he said.

What will become of my family, my wife, daughter, and son? What if I am caught? What will happen to them? I must leave here and go home to see them. How will I resettle completely into family life once having completed my current mission?

Did I really want to let the police know why I was killing he criminal scum? Was it guilt? Or was I always be looking for a reason to murder? To right the wrongs I had seen in the court system.

On returning home, I was able to contain myself after he first spree. However, the pent-up rage with those that thwart justice overtook me. "I tried. I held it in for years, but nothing changed. The evasion of justice by the guilty got worse", the cleaner screamed/

The justice system favoured the felon, not the victims. The perpetrators reside in society preying on people who try to follow the law. All each of those victims of these criminals got was grief, loss and often death.

I wish this had never started, but someone had to take control. Someone needed to stand up. If not me then who?

I can argue with myself the pros and cons of the motivation to kill. I find that I argue with myself about my thoughts and actions without ever reaching a conclusion or any resolution of my conflicted self."

 Now out loud with a singular audience of himself to witness his decision.

"I think I always wanted to kill. To avenge the wrong, I witnessed. To finalise the wrongs committed. As much as I might fool myself, I didn't really want to hand over the evidence to someone else, who would follow the law and only do not even a half good job, hamstrung by rules of law

Street Cleaner

and the need for a fair trial even though he accused, the guilty, did not offer that to their victims.

24. Day 4 - A rostered night off for the Cleaner?

Amy hoped that tonight was a night off for the Cleaner and maybe tomorrow as well. Surely everyone needed a rostered day off, even the most vengeful of killers. Tonight, thinking and talking about something other than the Cleaner.

Nor alone but with a charming dinner companion, who was easy on the eye to distract me from the day.

Dinner was enjoyable as was the company. Could he be the one who may move me with love in my every waking moments or is that just wishful thinking of those dating television shows which supposedly seek to match together people that are perfect for each other but who are often not?

Wasn't it normal to want a life other than work? Especially work such as I do. However, I have invested so much of myself in my work. Is there room for another life?

Her companion seeing Amy had become disengaged and had taken on a dream like state spoke, asked her "So do you think that the murder team will be where you would like to spend the next few years?" There was no immediate response from Amy.

"Amy, Amy" are you ok?

Street Cleaner

A distant voice was talking to Amy. She realised where she was and looked across at her dinner companion. "Sorry I was just thinking about the case", Amy lied. She had switched her thinking to dreaming of being the princess in a never-ending love story. At least she could dream.

She continued. "Yes, I feel that solving the most horrendous of cases is where I should be at this time. Maybe for ever. I am doing something to address the ultimate wrongs carried out on those people who can no longer address any wrongs, done to them or others. It's a people-oriented area of investigations. Investigating what people do to people. All of life/death, the bad and sometimes, though not often the good. My time earlier in fraud, mainly dealing with scammers and loan fraud was mostly all about numbers. People were involved but it was about the material, the movement of money not the personal."

Amy's dinner companion allowed her to continue until a natural lapse occurred in the conversation. "Dessert, he declared – I favour the bread and butter pudding a reminder of times past when it was made by my mother who seemed to turn bread that was going stale into a treat."

They had eaten well having shared a prawn curry with cumin rice entree, followed by him having the crusted lamb shoulder with beetroot salad while she had the lamb with fennel puree, parsnip chips and jus. No particular menu style was followed it was what each felt like, with an agreement to adventure a little in the food choices.

Amy considered dessert. Her hunger was fulfilled but she wanted the evening to continue. She had not been the best of companions with her mind drifting back to the events of the day and the days before. Her date had tried to be attentive and had taken a keen interest in her.

"I'll have the scented ice cream I think." stated Amy "The ice cream accompanied by thyme, honey, lemon and blueberry. However, I think the honey and blue berries will be enough. I think I will pass on the thyme and lemon. I want the sweet but not the sour. Sweet is what I enjoy most the herbs to the ice cream are like murders for a victim, bitter."

"They also seem out of place a night time meal" responded her companion.

Her companion passed on their orders to a waiter who looked just a little perturbed that there were changes to be made to a dish even if it was to leave off an accompaniment."

The ordering of the dessert allowed for each of them to retire to their respective "powder rooms" to as they say, freshen up.

The return of the couple to the table found their desserts waiting. Conversation continued with discussions of the niceties of life. Such as the favourite hotel they had each stayed in and favourite overseas trip. Amy found her companion was well travelled, though he said these were in the main business trips with accommodation he subsidised beyond the honorarium he was paid for accommodation to enjoy his time away.

Sometimes the tasks he had to perform when on these trips were unpleasant but at least the food and the hotels were more than pleasant. The discussion of the absence of overseas trips in Amy's work brought laughter though she did highlight some of her "over the water trips" to Wollongong and around Sydney. There was genuine laughter by both.

"Thank you", Amy said "this has been a lovely evening", with Amy surprised at how she had described the evening. Lovely was not a word she often the used. "We should ask for the bill."

As Amy turned to look for a waiter to let them know they had concluded their meal, her companion spoke "No need "he said" It has been covered."

"But I thought we were going to split it, "retorted, Amy, with a mixture of feigned protest and genuine happiness.

"Next time" he responded. Amy paused for a moment and then agreed "Next time."

She liked the idea there could, would, be a next time. That this had not been a one-time. She marvelled at there being a one-time let alone a possible next time, which had not happened to her for a long time. It was the fault of the job. There was the job and nothing but the job.

"Next time" she repeated. A small smile appearing on his face. Her companion also smiled at the idea of a next time.

The trip home together to her apartment was uneventful with chatter about the use of GPS systems to find you way, which were not always updated, resulting in people mindlessly driving into creeks. More laughter.

He walked her to the door of her building, took her gently and kissed her equally as gently.

"Till next time", she said, suddenly realising she was repeating herself as he walked away. For herself as the solo audience she whispered, "it was a lovely evening."

The glow on her face persisted until she opened her apartment door, entered, and saw her work clothes hanging ready for another day. The evening all but lost as her thoughts returned to the job, the pursuit of the Cleaner.

25. Day 5 – "No one will die today" – says Patrick-

Amy and Kalum saw the gates gracefully slide open. That is if large gates folding back almost noiselessly can be described as graceful. They parked in the designated area that had been described to them over the gate intercom. They had their credentials reviewed by a television camera at the locked gate obviously manned by some sort of guard within the house

A short pleasant walk to what Amy saw as a magnificent house. Kalum in particular took in all around him. Kalum and his wife were newish house owners in western Sydney. Looking for decorating ideas maybe.

Approaching the house, come office of Patrick Sliver it looked at first like many other large houses just out of a major city in Australia, both grand with a mixture of modern and old. Three floors could be distinguished from their view of the house exterior. Though there was no telling whether a cellar existed and what of the strange window in the centre of the roof. A wider than you might expect glass fenced balcony on the second floor seemed to wrap around the house with low level plants hanging over the balcony. There were no tall trees within around twenty metres of the house. A brick and stone design, built in what might be described as a cross between a ranch style, the old and a block style commercial building, the new. Grey in colour offset by a low-level garden featuring a variety of colourful plants with a begonia edge of varying colours on each separate garden bed.

Street Cleaner

As you got closer to the house you could see very small rectangular black boxes attached to the house near windows, which no doubt harboured cameras for a CCTV system. This was confirmed when they walked within approximately twenty metres of the building. You could see the front cover of each of the boxes noiselessly lift open with a camera emerging that settled on them and followed their journey from various angles up the path till they got close to the house. As they walked within ten metres of the door a slight movement occurred at one of the upstairs windows where a largish shadow appeared to partially open the window. The shadow appeared to be watching them as they closed in on the entry door.

The front door was opened by one of Silver's associates as they took their last few steps by to the door. They had been informed by the body-less voice at the gate to wait on the steps with no need to knock.

The door opening, with no need to wait indicated that their path was being closely monitored. The associate of African appearance, dressed in an open necked blue business shirt with a logo denoting Silver's organisation on the shirt and dark pants greeted them warmly and directed them inside.

The room into which they had been ushered was a large room to the right of the house entrance and reception area where they were invited to sit on a three-seat lounge. Sparkling mineral water with two glasses and two coffees had been placed on a coffee table placed in front of the lounge along with one Latte for Amy and a flat white for Kalum. How did Sliver's team know what types of coffee they each preferred? Scary! There was no sugar to be seen but neither, Amy nor Kalum took sugar.

A reception desk sat in the middle of the reception area. Further back from the house entrance to the left were people either with their heads down over computers or on the phone and/or looking at charts on the walls of where they worked. Most were young but some older faces seemed to be equally as busy as the bulk of the young staff that to Amy appeared to be under thirty-five years of age.

The furnishings in the room in which they waited featured wooden desks, wooden seats, and wood on the walls. Not just some sort of board imitating wood put up on the walls to look like a feature wall but genuine wood of different types. Some was Blackwood some was Boxwood, several panels from Gum trees and several varieties pf wood which could not be identified by Amy. The back of the large pen work room featured a glass door with what appeared to be an outside sitting area. Otherwise, there was no other glass. A total absence of windows gave the impression that the house and this room was a strategic command post, which in a way it probably was.

Coffee in hand the time passed pleasantly, with a series of television sets up on one wall to inform rather than entertain. Sky news, ABC 24, CNBC, BBC the featured channels. No need to watch the evening news or ever buy a newspaper again.

The young man who had met them at the door returned in what seemed like less than the ten-minute wait he had promised and announced that "Patrick, will see you now. No need to take your water as there is fresh water provided in Patrick's meeting space. You might like to take your coffee if you would like to finish it." Both had barely started their coffees "

They walked past a screen surrounding several desks of intense workers and up a single flight of stairs into a meeting area. More wood on the walls and in the furnishings. This time the floor was carpeted. Sitting in the grandest chair was Patrick Silver.

"Good morning" he said, casting aside the papers he gave the appearance of having been reading "I am Patrick" extending his hand to Amy and then to Kalum." Please take a seat. I think you will find the armchairs very comfortable." The chairs featured buttoned backs and sides, wide bases in a light green fabric which was comfortable to touch and even more comfortable to sit in. "To what do I owe this visit?"

Amy began. "We are investigating the murder cases of the killer dubbed the 'Cleaner'. Some of the news outlets have told us that your information service has provided them with information about the cases shortly before the time we received the information. Sometimes the media received the information an hour earlier, sometimes a half an hour earlier. We want to know what you know about the cases and how you seem to be in contact with the "Cleaner".

"Well," replied Patrick "it is disappointing that I appear to be only a half an hour ahead of you on some occasions. But you make a fair point there is no coincidence that I know what you know slightly ahead of you. One of our key businesses is set up to provide data and the processing of data into information so that people may apply the information to real world situations to create knowledge. We provide all sorts of data and information for a variety of users, law enforcement included."

"So do you know the Cleaner?" asked Kalum who through his tone showed he was not amused by this seemingly obvious self-promotion that Patrick had a reputation for undertaking at every meeting he attended.

"No. I don't know the Cleaner. But I can tell you that no one will die today. For some people that could be a pity. Though I don't share that sentiment. Life is precious. Every single life is precious, and none will fall by the Cleaner's hands today"

A pause took hold of the meeting during which you could hear the 'sound of silence'. A moment of consideration by Patrick of what he had just said. What Patrick had said was clearly being considered by Amy and Kalum. Who would speak next? Amy broke the silence.

"So how do you get the information your readership buys? Kalum asked"

"We derive our data and information for a variety of sources. The team conduct web searches of the Internet including sometime some searches on the dark web. In the cases you are asking about most of the time critical information comes from third parties. Some of it comes via email.

"Any other sources?" "On two occasions a person has visited me." Patrick went on. "Male, well his voice appears to have been male though it could be a deep voiced woman. The person wore a hoody, a surgical mask and a cap pulled down. I am pretty sure it was a male. He set up an arrangement for supplying us with information on your Cleaner" Silence.

Kalum continued. He was trying to disrupt the antics Patrick often used to delay getting to the point. It seemed to Kalum that Patrick was holding court, dishing out crumbs to a captive audience. Delighting in spinning the story his way for drawing kudos with an air of elitism he displayed in many public forums in which he spoke. Kalum wanted to get on the front foot and move along with the interview, so he tried to pepper Patrick with a series of short questions aimed at securing key facts quickly.

"Surely you can tell whether the person presented as a male or a female"?

Patrick paused again, a dramatic pause for the theatre, a moment of silence. "His face was covered. The hoody drawn down over his face. He also wore the mask and a cap. Some wisps of dark hair showed which appeared to be grown long. A jacket shirt and pants with no labels showing. Only his eyes were visible. They were green."

Kalum followed up with, "Any other key aspects of your visitor's description?"

"He was taller than me. I would say somewhere around 170cm to 180cm. Reasonable tan not the bottle type you find on most people. He stood up straight, walked confidently. He was maybe in his mid-thirties or slightly older."

"Clothes"?

Street Cleaner

After a short Patrick pause, "everyday trousers - chino look, light corn coloured, blue and white striped collared business shirt, clean but not polished black shoes and off course the hoody."

"Anything about his speech?"

"It appeared the person was well educated given what he said and how he spoke. Replied succinctly to questions after some thought was given to the answers he gave."

"Did he have a name?"

"He called himself Solomon. His name he believed was not important. He said his mission was to provide information to the public of what was to occur or had occurred with your Cleaner as quickly as possible. He claimed he was a representative of the Cleaner though he himself he said had never looked the Cleaner in the eye. I asked how he contacted the Cleaner and he demurred in his response. 'Nothing to tell' on that question was his response."

Patrick unusually seemed to be on a roll and continued without further prompting. "He visited me before the first killing. He also visited me just before the third killing. The first visit was to tell me of the coming of what he described as the cleansing of the streets, but he would not be pressed on details. Only that someone was coming to clean up the mess of what he termed as an ineffective justice system. By ineffective he meant that there was not much for the various perpetrators of crime under the current approach to carrying out he law to worry about as far as punishment goes, including white collar crimes to deter the criminals from their actions.

The second time was just before the third killing. He declined to give any more than a brief message on this occasion. The message was that tomorrow night the intentions of the Cleaner would now be obvious. The Cleaner as he was now being termed, was disappointed that the police had not made a connection between the first and subsequent murders (though he referred to cleansings rather than murders). This he claimed was worrying for the Cleaner as it appeared that people did not seem to be informed of his mission to clean the streets. ".

Patrick returned to his customary pause now having completed the information he was prepared to pass on. As Patrick had finished talking it seemed to Kalum that Patrick had lost interest in any further conversation.

"How did he get here? Did he make an appointment?" asked Kalum trying to restart Patrick's statement

Patrick seemed in an instant to have his interest rekindled. "I cannot say how he got here. He walked to the gate and up to the front door and away both times. I assumed he had a car parked somewhere on the road. Solomon stated at the end of both visits that if anyone followed him as he left he would transfer his allegiance to one of my competitors.

He made no appointment. The staff told me later that a call was received around 15 minutes before he arrived on both occasions to ask if I was in. When advised, the caller said thank you and hung up. I have listened to the calls, and it is

Street Cleaner

not the same voice as my visitor. It could have been his voice digitally altered or someone else made the call. We did not do an analysis of the voice. Too much time and cost for no real outcome. I will have one of our group email you a copy of the voice call. Our phone display showed no number"

"Do you think your visitor is the Cleaner?" asked Amy

Patrick paused. He seemed to be reflecting on his answers rather than establishing a dramatic moment through his silence.

"He could be", responded Patrick. "He was careful to always talk in third person and as I said he stated clearly that he had not looked the Cleaner in the eyes, which if it was the Cleaner is probably true. But my impression was that he was a messenger not the real thing"

Patrick went silent but suddenly stiffened in his char as if to advise Amy and Kalum that the meeting was now over.

"Can we get a copy of this email and previous emails? Amy was now anxious to review the words and have them analysed for any locational nuances. "We would also like the video of the meeting with sound as well as his arrival and departure. "

"It is an ok on the emails but a no on the video. If it was known that I had readily handed over a video of someone visiting me to the police, then this may turn future information sources off. If you succeed in obtaining a warrant, I will readily comply with some accompanying complaint to the media of police intrusion, big brother, and all that.

Two copies of the emails are printed and will be made available with a copy for each of you as you leave. This meeting is now over as I have work to do. I have already told you that there will be no death today. I can also tell you that the next victim will be a woman. An email arrived earlier today stating that street cleaning has no gender. It is about punishing those in society who hurt others regardless of who they are. Goodbye."

Patrick rose from his grand chair immediately after he finished speaking and disappeared through a previously concealed door. Amy and Kalum retraced their path back past the still intense workers, received the copies of the emails and continued out to their car.

Amy reviewed the emails as Kalum drove. The language was that of an educated person as Patrick had suggested. To Amy the words used, and the layout of each email was not any different to many emails she received or even to the emails she had written. The language couched in the form of a letter. The only possible unusual aspect of the emails was the spelling of the word program using the traditional English spelling of programme. The change of spelling to program from programme had started to become common usage at least thirty years ago. Solomon may be a traditional speller. Let the experts do their analysis.

The words Patrick had said were in the most recent email were clear on the page.

Street Cleaner

"The cleansing of the streets has no gender. It is about punishing those in society who bring hurt to others regardless of the form of that hurt and regardless of who may be hurt. The mission involves cleaning the streets. The next removal will be a woman who has brought pain to others, regardless of their circumstances and seems to continue to function almost with impunity. It will not happen today or even tomorrow but soon, very soon."

26. Meeting at six - "So what do we know?"

"We have had another reminder to look out for our esteemed adversary. At the moment the odds of finding out who is the felon are not as good, as knowing that Caine killed Abel. Only two of them with one having the motive means and opportunity. In our one killer, with a not completely unknown but seemingly unclear motive there is certainly the possibility of many opportunities through means at their disposal.

No brother sneaking up on another in these cases. No one to be a brother's keeper. At least it seems clear there is only one person for us to deal with.

Let's make it a short meeting after another long day. There is not much more for me to say, except that at least no one died to today."

Bible concluded his introductory remarks.

So, what else do we know? Amy?"

"Well we have firmed up our profile of the person we are seeking. Aerial and Johnathan can you tell us what you have been doing. This alerted the young detectives to describe their meetings with Apollo and Caroline as well as the meeting with Dr. Davina that some present had missed. The new deceves took everyone through the new profile.

Amy took the group through the meeting that she and Kalum had with Patrick, including that the Cleaner had gone from apparently an opportunist to a planned killer and the existence of the mysterious Solomon. The announcement that the next victim almost certainly was likely to be a woman was greeted by murmurs amongst the group and questions as to how a woman might figure in the Cleaner's thinking.

Amy responded "Women are not an exception in the world of crime, with Sydney notables such as the 'war' between Kate Lee and Tilley Devine fighting to control of the sex trade and other vices in the early 20th century. However, we need to investigate as to what women are currently running criminal enterprises which seems to be a common link between the criminals killed so far."

Amy fielded the, who, what, where and when questions on the possible women who might be a target. "It may be that the Cleaner will look beyond organised criminal enterprise to individuals who have committed a crime, possibly an intentional crime or even a non-intentional crime.

For instance, there are major road accidents where multiple deaths occur because of tiredness, speed, drugs, and alcohol. Some women have defrauded their bosses. I heard of one woman who invited her boss to Christmas drinks at the house owned by her and her husband. The boss knew what he paid the woman and the approximate salary her husband a teacher commanded and was surprised by the size and quality of the house in which the couple lived. The employee had always demonstrated she could competently arrange banking, dealing with audits and settling tax affairs.

The Boss had a new external auditor come in and review a variety of transactions over the twenty years she had been working for her boss. After reviewing three random years it was clear that the woman had stolen at least $500,000 using fake and duplicate invoices. Up till then he had left the financial side of the business to her and through her actions she took the some of the profits of the business from him.

So much potential for what people term white collar crime. Solicitors' trust funds, Ponzi schemes, bank fraud, computer viruses holding an organisation to ransom, and in this case duplicate accounting records. An endless array of potential individual crimes, which often see very lenient punishments. No one hurt. Not likely.

Amy went on. "We are undertaking a search of women who have committed major crimes in the last five years such as car accidents causing a death, fraud in excess of twenty-five thousand dollars, multiple nursing home deaths where carers may have been suspected of being involved etc. We hope to turn up some useful names"

We will also be reinterviewing Patrick Silver whose independent information servicing business has been getting news of the actions of the Cleaner and selling the stories on to the media at the same time or earlier than we are aware of a death.

After a pause "Dismissed, enjoy your night" yelled Bible or "the return to work for some. For those of us returning to our work, may your dedication to your work see you rise up as if you were eagles to seek - the truth?" An upward intonation in the final two words maybe questioned the current efforts of some. He had deliberately adapted a quotation from the book of Isiah in the Old Testament section of the Bible to add rhyme to the finish of his conclusion to the meeting.

With the final words hitting the ears of those people working on, a little muttering could be heard as they slumped away.

27. Day 6. "Maybe a breakthrough"

Aerial had been assigned the task of going over all the evidence to date. Reviewing documents ensuring key facts were listed on white boards and summarised into meaningful files.

Such things as the post-mortem turned up with nothing of interest. Apart from the first victim, all the victims had been shot with the same gun. The forensic investigation had also not turned up anything of note. Nothing unusual on the emails, apart from the spelling that Amy had noted which came from a proxy sever that had been deleted

Aerial wondered how these CSI type shows managed to turn up evidence which then leads to the identification of a suspect. Aerial was an avid watcher of a British drama where a private team of coroners and forensic investigators would always find a strand of fabric or some abnormality on or in the body which would lead them to a breakthrough and the capture of the killer in a short period of time.

The coroner on another British program had limited resources and time as she doubled as a local doctor. The doctor providing little more than the likelihood that the deceased had been murdered and how they are likely to have been murdered. The case(s) reminded Aerial of some of the cases on this program.

After all the witness statements and background information had been tallied and cross-checked Aerial sat thinking through what she had done, assessing whether anything had been missed. As she thought through what she had done, she heard what seemed to be distant sound. Only it wasn't distant as she realised when she awoke from a trance, brought on by the deep penetrating tiredness she now felt and her concentration on the information in front of her. It was the maker installed ringtone of her mobile.

"Aerial speaking". "Hi Aerial, Johann here, just following up on the phone, internet etc. from the case you are working on." Johann was a specialist analyst inside the police force who dealt with breaking through firewalls and analysing electronic equipment. Always a pleasant and cool person when Aerial had dealt with him in her prior uniform roll.

"There is nothing new on any of the phones of the victims. Call register for the month before they died appears to be family and a few friends apart from those criminal contacts that you already had. I will email over the list. However, the reason I rang is that the emails going to Patrick Silver appear to be coming from the one location. Though the emails seemingly show up overseas locations, they appear to be originating in Australia. It seems to be originating from Coopernook."

"Coopernook?" responded Aerial quizzically.

"Yes" went on Johann "I looked it up. It is small town of less than 600 hundred people, twenty-four kilometres north of Taree, which was pushed off the Pacific Highway when a diversion road was built some years ago.

Apparently, there is an NBN provider in the area who advertises high speed internet. I have not found the exact location. It appears to be around the Macquarie Street, George Gibson Drive and Ridge Streets in the town, if there is town. The map shows that the 'town' looks more like a village. The send location seems to move in that area. It seems like, a laptop on the move hooking into unsecured web providers. The URL used each time differs though there is the repeat use of some of them. There is a school in the area in particular which has been accessed. Also, a hotel and several small stores seem to be being used as portals. Only six in total but it is a small town.

 The sender has only used apparently different 'bogus' email accounts mostly hot mail accounts. Once used and then abandoned. I wanted to let you know before I email everything which I should have packaged up and sent to you to arrive early tomorrow. I have some other work to do tonight"

"Thanks Johann, best news of the day. I owe you. Talk again soon." She hung up without waiting to hear a goodbye. A lift in spirits, sudden quickening of thought. A lead, maybe.

Aerial discussed this new information audibly with herself. "I wonder if this will provide us with a breakthrough, if the transfers can be linked to this Solomon that may in turn lead us to his employer, if he has one and onto the Cleaner." Hopefully this does not turn out to be a peripheral issue and not mean much to the current case."

"Hi" said Aerial when she was answered by Amy's voice mail. "Nothing new apart from Johann over in tech who found that the emails to Patrick Silver's account each of which originates from URL's in Coopernook in NSW.

Street Cleaner

I will have everything completed including the tech report by early tomorrow. Maybe a breakthrough. Talk soon."

The return call came quickly, less than five minutes. There was no hello. "Best news we have had all day," came from Amy down the phone. "I want you and Johnathan to go to Coopernook tomorrow. Leave the final report if you not yet finished. You should pack a bag. It is a long car trip". Aerial never got to speak apart from ok and will do before Amy was gone.

Clearly no plane? Aerial sent an SMS to Johnathan, with all the basic details which Amy had let him know was coming which he read at the small café while waiting for a meal, after a shopping trip.

He replied, "Nothing like a drive in the country. Meet you at six at work. I think it will take more than two nights, given the drive there and back. I will take the first 300km. I am about to book some accommodation" Johnathan messaged back.

Aerial packed up for the day. The final finishing work on the report can wait till after we get back. If I have to be back in at 6 its time for me to leave. Nothing like a field trip although, Coopernook does not sound like my normal vacation territory.

28. Day's 6 to 8 – Coopernook or bust

Coopernook is a small town. More like the size of a village. Three hundred and thirty kilometres from Sydney. A four-to-five-hour drive.

It is said that the name Coopernook is translated form the local indigenous language Birip as "elbow". The elbow for Coopernook is the bend in the nearby Lansdowne River that passes the town. The town used to be on the main road to Brisbane, the Pacific Highway. But earlier this century a bypass was built which meant the town is now off the highway. The reason for the establishment of the town is unclear, though it had logging in its past and the river could have carried the logs to larger locations to the south and south west of the town. The Primary School was established in 1876 one year before the Coopernook post office and has an enrolment of less than 80 children.

Aerial and Johnathan set off on their trip just after 6:00AM (0600). Johnathan was taking the first driving shift. He suggested Aerial take over after the second coffee stop with the first one to be at the next drive through take away they saw.

They would both be staying at the Hotel Coopernook. The other accommodation in town was a B and B and a motel with both not having any available accommodation on the days they were to stay. Three days had been booked in, given messages only came to Patrick Silver from Coopernook no more than every second day and never before 3.00. If needed they could extend their stay. They wanted to be sure that they had covered all possible time frames in case the sender broke the regular pattern of transmission.

Aerial readily agreed with the arrangements made and while Johnathan started the drive, she summarised what she had found out about Coopernook. She also went through a short summary of the key Internet users in Coopernook. It was always going to be a short list as though Wi-Fi existed in Coopernook it was at a premium. Some messages had come from a park using as a hot spot the school WI-FI It had been used on several occasions. The hotel and the local lock up appeared to be other Internet sources used. All were likely sources that could be used for further messages to Patrick Silver. With a population of 538 at the 2016 census, which had grown to 625 as at the 2021 census though a growing population this was always going to be a small town which could likely be covered easily.

One they cleared the city which took nearly two hours the countryside featured unkempt bushland as you might expect in the Australian countryside. The Australian bush was always found in its natural state. No Black Forest here. In general, the Australian bush, scrub with gum trees and a few other local and imported species, grew, lived, and then died mostly with little water to keep it in any great shape only to rise again with the next big rain event or as a result of a bushfire releasing new seeds for future growth.

The plan was clear. They would let Johann know when they were within a short distance of Coopernook. He would begin to monitor messages going to the email addresses that Patrick Silver had set up. Johann knew that he needed to break in again to the Silver network as Silver had blocked his previous entry route. But as Johann said every blockage provides a new entry point. Neither Silver nor Johann discussed these blockages or break in's though they both knew they occurred. No warrant had been issued. There was just an implicit understanding that Johann would break in and Silver once aware of the break in would block the entry point.

After a coffee and food stop around three hundred kilometres into the journey, they were now within thirty or so kilometres of Coopernook. The road was quiet, with few cars or trucks on the highway. Johnathan had contacted Johann who was now monitoring all possible links between Silvers computers and those in Coopernook. Aerial had taken over the driving for the last stretch of the journey.

It was now after eleven approaching midday as they entered the town proper. The decision to drive rather that to fly to Taree and pick up a car had been to minimise any possible noticeable activity that may have alerted the local population. As it had for centuries, news travelled fast in the bush, with or without the use of the internet.

The Hotel Coopernook appeared to be like its picture that appeared on the web. Booking in was straight forward and though each of their rooms could not be described as stylish they proved to be clean and tidy, with comfortable beds. The hotel was one street back from the main street of the town, which meant it was one street back from the local police station.

Amy had suggested that it was a courtesy to let the local police know you were carrying out an investigation in town.

Otherwise, they should lay low, giving any locals they encountered the story that they were real estate agents looking for a small property for a Sydney racehorse owner to buy to spell some of their horses from time to time, but this was just one of the locations they were looking at and nothing had been decided.

Johnathan had nothing so far from Johann, but it was still early to expect a message to be sent. There was traffic on the line but nothing useful to the case. Around 2:45 it was mutually agreed they should get back in the car and cruise through the town via the main street, Macquarie Street.

A few people were about. The school was coming out. The Coopernook general store posted with an old four-square sign offered seven day take away food and included a news agency. A few children were dropping in once they left school. Nothing outstanding was happening.

Johnathan and Aerial waited in their car on Macquarie Street appearing to be looking at strip maps of roads in the area. At 3:15 a call from Johann. An email had been sent to Silver from near the school on Macquarie Street or at least using their Wi-Fi. It said it was definitely a woman who would be next on the list. Someone who stole from others and got off with a light sentence was next.

Still on Macquarie Street, Aerial u-turned the car sharply and headed in the direction of the school, just seconds away. Several cars were making pickups at the school. It was a question of which car. Only one car was not making a pickup and was now pulling out of the curb not quickly but not at a parent pace. The car passed the school as Johnathan and Aerial were approaching the school.

Johnathan had been taking a picture off all cars and as many people in Macquarie Street as possible, but it appeared the black Holden Barina, a few years old, given General Motors had stopped producing local cars some years ago and discontinued selling any cars in Australia a few years after production stopped looked like it could be a likely source of the transmission. They drove slowly going forty metres or so past the school and making another u turn, then picked up speed in the direction of the Barina. Once they were close enough but not on top of the departing car, Johnathan noted the registration number and rang to identify the owner. A local owner and a local address, neither of which meant anything to Johnathan or Aerial.

Johnathan had established the car belonged to a local, Geoff Greenaway who was heading back to the Pacific Highway. Is this Solomon? The thought crossed both their minds. "It is too far from Sydney to be, the Solomon", mused Johnathan as Aerial piloted the car. She was driving a safe distance behind the departing vehicle.

Back on the highway and heading north, the car turned onto a minor street around ten kilometres from Coopernook. Aerial slowed their car so as not to turn at the same time as the Barina. This was not a chase. It was clear the car being followed had not been interested in anyone pursuing them.

The Barina pulled into a driveway which appeared to have sheds and a homestead around two kilometres up a well-defined track from the main road. With nowhere else to go,

Aerial followed the car onto the property with a sudden increase in urgency. Johnathan drew his service revolver given they did not know what to expect.

Both cars came to a dusty stop with Aerial swinging inside the other vehicle, creating swirls of dust. As Aerial stopped, Jonathan swung out of the car with all the dexterity of Bruce Willis who in one film had left the car while it was still moving, aiming, and firing his weapon with consummate accuracy. Johnathan did not try to mimic such athleticism, nor did he fire at the man now getting out of his car.

Johnathan had made a quick exit though not as sensational but equally effective. He had his police identification out and his gun raised, while at the same time announcing to the man, they assumed was Geoff Greenway that they were police. He ordered the surprised man to place his hands on the bonnet of his car.

If this was the "Cleaner or even Solomon", neither Aerial nor Johnathan was taking any chances. Aerial with her gun now drawn joined Johnathan watching the now puzzled and worried looking man. The apparent lack of urgency by the man to comply with instructions prompted Aerial to yell "up against the car." Johnathan cast a sideways look at Aerial who was not prone to yelling and screaming even at delinquent suspects but a small smile across his lips conceded that her approach to encouraging the suspect to comply would get a response, which it did.

After Aerial's ultimatum the man seemed to suddenly realise that this was serious and almost slapped his hands down as he placed them on his car. A quick frisk by Johnathan showed no concealed weapons. As he finished the weapons check Jonathan suggested "that we might go inside and have a chat about some messages you have been sending."

29. Is Geoff the Cleaner?

A search of the now shaking man had revealed no weapons. The house was clear. The three now sat in the lounge area of a ranch style house. The furnishings a mixture of old and contemporary. The three were facing each other, with Aerial and Johnathan sitting on a new three-seater lounge. Geoff faced them in what was clearly a favourite old lounge rocker.

Geoff was a fit looking man who appeared to be in his early sixties, dressed casually but in well-cut quality clothes. His hair was starting to go silver grey. His manner was agitated, which was to be expected but he seemed to be aware of the situation he confronted though he was confused as to why these police were in his house.

Aerial led off "Geoff Greenway", in the search for weapons Johnathan had happened upon the suspect's wallet. The name of the registered owner of the car was the same as the one found on the current license.

Aerial had lapsed back into her everyday voice. "We believe you have been assisting the murderer, known as the Cleaner in carrying out a strong of crimes. Such assistance could make you liable for..."

"Now wait a minute", roared back Greenway, half rising as he began yelling. "I don't know this cleaner; I have never met him. I don't know anything about him." Johnathan also now half standing motioned for Greenway to sit and calm himself.

Aerial continued, "Did you not send an email by tapping into an internet connection in the main street of town within the last 30 minutes? You broke the law by using a private network without permission"

Greenway paused. Aerial and Johnathan paused. "Yes, that is true. I don't know who owns the email account. But I do send messages from time to time. Just messages. I am instructed where to be and how to logon to an available network. I don't know who owns the network ". He paused.

Johnathan stepped up his voice this time. "So, you sent it. How did you know the message to send? Who asked you to send the message and the other messages you have sent before today? Did you get paid to do this or is it just your noble character shining through helping a friend? Don't make us ask every single question. Just tell us what is going on."

Greenway's eyes opened a little wider. "It started some time ago when a man called of all things Solomon was visiting the town. I met him at the pub. He seemed like an educated one and was able to talk about a variety of topics. His face was always partially covered with a hoody, which he said was due to scars he had as a result of an industrial accident that he did not want people to see. He felt uncomfortable about his appearance. This Solomon was looking for someone to send messages to someone in Sydney. Apparently, he was working with someone else on some land deal and some other business who could not send them direct as there was a question of an old conflict between the parties, one of which he said lived locally in the Coopernook area.

For each message I am sent, $250 in cash arrived in the mail box with the message to be sent. I was told I would be using different Internet providers each time. This would help conceal the source of the message. I have some skills in that area" He stopped talking.

"Did this not appear to you to be a suspicious way to carry on", followed up Aerial. "It did ", said Greenway. "He, Solomon said if I was not happy to send a particular message, I should not send it. However, the messages appeared to be in code. I can get todays for you"

Greenway left the room. Johnathan stood followed and watched as Greenway went into a room that appeared to be a study. Aerial and Johnathan without speaking were coming to the same view, that Geoff Greenway, was not, Solomon or the Cleaner, just an old bloke picking up some spare cash.

Geoff Greenway returned with an A4 sheet of paper with a short message typed close to the centre of the page.

4WoSyd2d3d.

It was clear to both officers that the message was about murder number 4. It was to be a woman; it was to occur in Sydney and it was to occur in two to three days. "And you don't know what this means?" asked Johnathan as he secured the message in with his case notes.

"No" replied Greenway, "I did not link the messages to anything other than a somewhat strange and sociable man trying not to have a message linked back to him. I thought it might be a code for stock market information. The messages have been turning up in my mailbox from time to time over the last few weeks. I don't think they are posted as there is never a stamp"

"Geoff, do you have the original message and the envelope?" said Johnathan "No mate, tore it up and it was collected on garbage night.

"Alright", continued Johnathan. "If another message arrives, you are not to send it. It is be taken to the local police station. If the message comes in an envelope then unopened. As my colleague was saying before you jumped up, your involvement could be considered as an accessory before the fact. You may have to face the same penalty as the killer. We are not laying charges today, but we will be informing the local station of your possible involvement in a crime. They will be visiting from time to time to check you are still living here. Do you live alone?'

"No replied Greenway, "the family is away, my wife and our youngest grandchild who is living with us are away for two days while his parents are overseas working for two more weeks. Our Grandson normally lives in Newcastle." Goodbyes were said. A final warning about any future messages. A caution not to leave the area. Business cards given to Greenway with contact numbers for Aerial and Johnathan.

"He is definitely not the Cleaner and not Solomon" Johnathan mumbled to himself but loud enough for Aerial to hear.

A visit to the local police as a courtesy and to enlist their help in looking in on Greenway without explaining what case they were working on. An overnight stay but the second night was no longer needed with an early start the following morning.

The trip was now in reverse, back to Sydney. They knew the hotel did not have any interior cameras and were aware that Geoff Greenway would not have let anyone else know what he was doing to protect his nice side earner. They discussed their findings with Amy by phone and emailed their notes of the interview they had conducted.

They soon cleared the Coopernook area but not before a man with a hoody waiting in the bush not far from the turn off to Geoff Greenway's watched them depart Coopernook. Almost invisible to anyone looking in his direction, the man was using high powered binoculars to watch Johnathan and Aerial leave town. No one arrested he thought. The end of messages going through this channel. Time to get back to Sydney.

Part 5 A Woman to die? More than one?

30. Day 8 Amy and the Cleaner make contact.... almost

I am sure you know that when you work in a large city you are bound to sometimes bump into other people you know or people who know you that you don't know. Most people are just faces or not even that, bodies you pass, you brush against, you navigate around. Not really people but obstructions. Occasionally there is a collision.

With Aerial and Johnathan out of town and Kalum at a "personal meeting" which he had been somewhat secretive about, Amy took an hour in her ten-hour day to go up town and eat some different food from that found around work and enjoy a walk.

The Cleaner had similar thoughts.

Pitt Street Plaza a closed off roadway in Sydney where shop rents are the third most costly in the world can be busy around an extended lunchtime, (12 till 2) on any day. Today there was street theatre. A small young woman with an Irish accent had drawn a sizeable crowd through her promise to squash her body into a small plastic box. In her rhetoric, she stated more than once that the box was one metre by one metre by one metre. One cubic metre. For this feat she sought and received the promise of the crowd that each of them would stay till the end of the performances and would reward her with more than one gold coin each or better still folding money. No silver please. Just gold or notes. A final emphasis being that this is how I make a living. "I do not get any subsidy, no payments. I am dependent on you wonderful looking, gracious people for the means to buy my daily bread."

Amy found herself watched what appeared to be an agonising process as the performer seemed to contort her body and seemingly disconnect some of her body parts from each other so that she might be able to fit into the box. Her movement seemed fluid at one moment and then jerky as the woman, twisted and turned her body in pursuit of her goal and her subsequent reward, a sea of paper money she wished for from the crowd. No silver, and if it has to be gold then several please and only the higher denomination.

The Cleaner who liked to kill but at the moment was killing time, was by chance in the same area eating a salad roll from a brown paper bag. He like others joined the circle that had formed around the performer, watching the act while on occasion glancing around the crowd. Only once the body stuffing show had begun, did the Cleaner spot Amy. He was not looking for her, she just appeared. He averted his glare once he had caught sight of her, not wanting to stand out. He pulled out a pair of prescription sunglasses, for enhancing images in the distance, from his pocket so he might get a better look at the person he now considered his nemesis without being noticed. Though he was on the shady side of the plaza he was not out of place in donning his sunglasses. Walking in sunglasses outdoors and for some people both in and out of doors was a style requirement, regardless of the weather.

Street Cleaner

Amy appeared to the Cleaner to be enchanted by the show. She clapped loudly when the woman was able to push, her body into the small box. With a sense of excitement generated by the show, Amy would rush as she thought so would most of the crowd, who had stayed for the theatre to make good on the crowd promise of much gold or fold.

The Cleaner would also come forward with his contribution towards the entertainer buying her delayed bread. He was less interested in the success of the promised show, though he appreciated the theatre, and more interested in getting closer to Amy.

"A risk" he said without sound. Thoughts went quickly through his mind as he followed others forward to the performer who had put out the traditional hat out to collect her reward. "Is it worth the risk of being recognised or should I just see If she really knows who I am?" The Cleaner silently said to himself"

Though, each of them approached from a different direction, their paths seemed to bring them closer together. For the Cleaner it was intentioned movement. For Amy there was no intent. It seemed that a secret magnet was leading her to an encounter with the Cleaner. An unplanned encounter. Someone who knew her that she did not know.

Suddenly the Cleaner felt something touching his back. He and everyone else seemed not to have realised that what had been a silent chase, or at least not one was shouting, by a group of people, store staff, as well as plain clothes police of what turned out to be a young felon who had apparently stolen something from a nearby store was about to crash into the crowd.

The chasers had been waiting for the young felon to leave the shop. Apparently, the thief recognised one of the plain-clothes female cops and the chase was on.

The young man inadvertently ploughed into the Cleaner and other audience members as he tried to make his escape. The chase was no longer silent. The young man in turn was pushed by someone, who took offence at being pushed and in turn pushed back. Action had begun close to the Cleaner. In no time the silent chase gained audio with someone giving the loud and expected call of- "Stop thief."

The felon stumbled and fell. The Cleaner had become distracted from his newly created goal, which was to watch Amy watching the show. He was being pushed along with the chase joining the suddenly enlivened crowd and was heading unbeknown to both he and Amy for a momentary collision with Amy.

At the last moment someone else provided a counter action. A universal principal. For every action there is a reaction. This counter action, by an unknown crowd member was to push the felon back towards the way he had come. The felon fell again onto the Cleaner but managed to retain his feet though he was not going anywhere given the density of people around him. He had reversed direction from the original push but was definitely not going anywhere.

The Cleaner though was clearly unstable and was beginning to fall. As he went down, he tried to push back. The crowd changed focus from watching the entertainer collecting her reward to the disturbance a new source of entertainment. Crowd focus was now centred on the area where the Cleaner appeared to be a central character in a mixture of the original crowd, the felon and the chasing throng.

The new focus of the original crowd was towards him, well at least in his direction. Not being able to stand any longer under the weight of the thrust of the people one way and then the other he fell and took down the felon along with a small woman and a man whose stomach clearly preceded him. In a twist the Cleaner unbeknown to those around him as a violent criminal became one of the crowd figures who were applauded for catching the thief.

Amy and the Cleaner had avoided an unplanned meeting, though Amy of course did not know the meeting was to occur or in fact that the Cleaner was near her. The Cleaner regained his feet as uniformed bicycle police who had followed the chasing pack seemed to be conducting their own version of a melee in their attempt to grab at the young thief who now was on the ground but still trying to crawl away. Our thief was injured now with blood coming from a head cut. The uniformed police took charge of the situation. Captured!

Amy came forward and identified herself as a police officer to the pursuing group now holding the thief. The story was short that they gave to Amy. Though they all appeared fit, there is always recovery after any run. As breath settled the undercover female cop said they were staking out the store as the thief, was a regular non-paying customer of the store and other stores around. The local police who were waiting in an adjacent street had been briefed and who within a moment of the pursuit beginning had appeared on the scene on their bicycles. It was all under control, now. Amy complimented the fellow police officers on their actions, and then everyone went their separate way. The crowd was now drifting off though some people were chatting to each other. Strangers a few minutes ago now bonded together by a shared experience reliving not just one source of lunch time entertainment but two theatre events.

The Cleaner now wounded with a few scratches as souvenirs of his venture into central Sydney began to make his way back through the departing crowd. I took a chance he thought which nearly turned bad. " Stupidity" he said to the listening audience of just one, himself. Silently continuing to chastise himself, he walked away from the scene at a measured pace, disciplining himself, not to look back.

As the crowd dispersed, a small woman with an Irish accent shouted, "Hey don't forget your promise - gold or fold."

31. Nothing happened till -Day 12 then Number 4 – Angela Bates

Nobody died for three days. But it didn't last.

Angela Bates, former solicitor and convicted embezzler recently released from prison on parole lay dead in an unlit area in Darling Harbour on Cockle Bay. Once predominantly a freight rail train yard the area now boasted the International Convention Centre (ICC), a shopping centre with a tourist bent, restaurants, parks, a Chinese Garden in attraction a zoo, an aquarium, and a local Madam Tus Saud's.

Behind the binding framed by a several garbage containers, covered in cardboard which was to be recycled a body was hidden so as not to be easily seen from the street or by passers-by. Under the cardboard, some of which had blown away lay the body of the dear departed Angela Bates. She was found by an excited cleaner, (not The Cleaner), who seemingly had little working knowledge of English but who seemed to be keen on the word dead. The response "She dead, when I found her", was his answer to most all the questions he was asked." Several other people also arrived momentarily at the scene of the discovery, walking through the area on an early journey to work.

Angela Bates was found around 5:40 AM or 0540 as those within the group with military service insisted on given the 24-hour clock had, been ingrained into them. There had been media suggestions that Australia should switch to the 24-hour clock and then the relentless teaching of time, with AM and PM, often without effect in schools could be eliminated from the curriculum freeing up time for the many other areas of learning teachers had become responsible for, from the last decades of the twentieth century till now. The organised and a few social media stars pushed this agenda till it lost the interest of the public. All of three days.

As Amy drove to the scene her mind wandered to the various media pushes for everything from the so called simplifying of telling the time to whether there should be gender equality for the position of Prime Minister. A woman then a man. What of those people now had recorded on their birth certificates, where state law allowed, as not having a gender? Do they get a rotation?

Given almost every person had access to social media and saw themselves either as a crusader or a journalist, with some people believing they were both news services and social reformer had the news earlier than the police. Representatives of the organised media, both commercial and government owned who continued to try to maintain their relevance to the community, the consumers of their news by pushing out all sorts of ideas on how to govern the country, manage education, how to penalise polluters and how business should redeem the environment as well as a series of freelancers started arriving on the scene within minutes of the find. They could be heard discussing angles on this latest killing as they set up equipment ready to broadcast. The police were not slow they arrived and began cordoning off the scene as the first journalist arrived.

The members of the fourth estate competed against at the scene for space with the large usually untrained swill of influencers and news hounds that used the internet to pursue all manner of agendas, not least of which was individual personal fame and fortune. A new profession had been created that of an influencer, which was so called legitimate work. Amy had no time to consider the merits of this newish form of employment. Her mind was sharply brought to the task at hand as she drove passed signs that said "No vehicular Entry" into Darling Harbour and yet another of the Cleaner's murder scene.

Another early awakening. She shuddered though not cold as she approached the job at hand. Angela Bates. Another person was dead.

Amy and Kalum were both on the scene well within 30 minutes of the reported find as they both had been coming in early to discuss with Aerial and Johnathan their discoveries at Coopernook.

'At first glance this killing looks like the others. Shot twice on this occasion, once in the shoulder and probably a second shot to the forehead, close to the middle", suggested Kalum. Nothing appears to be much different. The only differences between the various murders/ assassinations, is that some, certainly this one, have a second wound other than the head shot. The way she fell sprawled out, appeared possibly she was trying to flee. This could mean she knew the killer."

"Who found the body?" Kalum stopped talking waiting for a response from the uniform police at the scene. Amy having had arrived from the north and also asked attending police who had called in with the find? "A variety of people" said a sergeant now speaking to both of them, "came upon the scene at around the same time. A cleaner whose only words were when I spoke to him, "she dead when I found her and I see nothing" as well as several others who said they had not heard any shots. Jennifer Cleary who works in a building nearby called it in on 000. She has stayed at the scene, though would be happy to get away as soon as possible as her boss is not particularly understanding if she is not in by 7:00. We picked the victim's bag off the ground. Licenses inside identified her as Angela Bates. Gloves of course "

"Ok then let's talk to her, we can't have an unhappy boss waiting for his morning coffee, just because a murder has been committed." Amy was speaking while heading off in the direction where Kalum had pointed to where Jennifer was standing while the Sergeant had been passing on his information.

Amy addressed a woman shorter than herself around forty with what Amy would describe as a good dress sense. "I understand you are Jennifer and you called it in, and you have an intolerant boss"." "Yes" replied the woman "I am Jennifer Cleary and you are right. The boss can be somewhat intolerant if everyone is not in when he gets there." Jennifer went on with a half-smile" particularly me as I am the Operational Manager of the business. I wasn't the only one there. A man was shouting 'She dead', who when he saw me said 'I see nothing'. Several other people rushed to the scene. A second or so after I arrived. They had to get to get to work. For those who were willing I took pictures of their driver licenses. Each person was happy to discuss what they heard and saw but wanted to be on time for work, maybe there is more than one intolerant boss. I agreed to stay with the dead woman."

Street Cleaner

Amy admired the organisation and forethought of this woman. "Thanks for staying and getting details on other witnesses. We will need to get a statement in the future but for now if you could just tell us what you heard and saw."

"I was walking from the car park when I heard the two shots. Two people in front of me looked around not knowing the source or the direction of the noise, earphones in, but the shots were loud enough for them to hear it. I hurried past them as I recognised the noise as shots as I have been pig shooting with my father who lives in the central west of the state. At the same time, I heard the accented voice saying "She dead, she dead

A man in black coat bumped me as I came around the back of the car park. As well as wearing a black coat, he had on his feet what looked like military boots. Under the coat was a blue business shirt. His face was obscured by a hat that was pulled down, but I could see he had a bronze tan, probably fake as it seemed to be evenly spread on the lower side of his face that was not obscured. I do not see any more of his face. His hands came out of his pockets as he steadied himself after bumping into me and he offered a "sorry" as he moved on quickly. Only one word was spoken. No discernible accent. I do not know which way he went. I did not realise that he could be connected to the shooting. I was focussed on getting to where I heard the shot. Afterward I realised that he may have been or had seen the shooter. I found the woman. The two people I passed on the way round arrived at the scene in seconds as I was phoning you lot. That's it.

"Any chance you would recognise him again", Kalum asked" as a follow up to the concise observations of Jennifer.

Jennifer thought for a moment. "Unlikely, I did not see enough of his face. Just the bottom section, mouth and chin, a half-moon shaped mouth as you might see in an emoji, strong, prominent though not pointy chin, the skin evenly tanned. No distinguishing marks"

"Well observed" commented Amy. "I know you need to get away. Can you send me a copy of the details you took from the other witnesses and a description of anyone who declined as well as a photo of your license?" Amy handed her a card that listed her details, while thinking we should be able to recruit people like this Jennifer. "Someone will be in touch to get you to come in and give a written statement. And thank you for your efforts at the scene. Your boss can call me or my Sergeant Kalum, who was also passing on a card if there are any problems." A rare moment with all three of the group smiling

Kalum and Amy inspected the body. There was nothing new to see and nothing new to know. It was the Cleaner with the number four wrapped around the victim's bag.

Why had Angela Bates been meeting someone so early in the morning? The report had come in around in within ten minutes of the shooing. Her wallet contained her driver's license, which had a picture showing a recent likeness to the corpse that had once been a woman. The license of course included an address.

xxxxxxxxxxxxxxxxxxxxxxxxxxxxxxxxxxxxxxxxxxxxxxxxxxxxxxxxxxxx
xxxxxxx

Street Cleaner

After a final review of the scene, next stop was the address on the license. It turned out to be a semi in Balmain. A younger version of Angela Bates answered the door. Resemblance to the real Angela was uncanny. A cliché but not untrue in this instance.

"We are from the police, does Angela Bates live here?" Their identification cards made it obvious to the younger version of Angela Bates that they were police. The double replied almost immediately laying out several facts without the need for any penetrating questions. "Yes, she does. She is my mother. I am Kathryn Reiner, nee Banks, though I prefer to be called K, just the letter K, rather than Kathryn. She has been living here in a one-bedroom studio at the back of the property which I own with my husband. I guess this is bad news, so please come in and take a seat."

Amy and Kalum entered a tastefully decorated lounge area with the walls were painted in pastels. The furnishings were stylish and clearly chosen to match the décor of the house. An adjoining room showed a chic kitchen, complete with all the appliances you see described in the three-million-dollar range of houses.

Off to the side of the kitchen was an indoor, outdoor room. Amy recognised a Nolan on the walls. Was it a good print? Maybe it was an original painting? The seating was comfortable, too comfortable, the view of the kitchen disappeared as Amy and Kalum sank into the furnishings. Oh, to live like this thought Kalum to himself.

"We have some bad news", started Kalum, who noticed Amy was still taking in all the furnishings around her. "Oh yes what has mummy done this time?" responded K.

"Unfortunately, your mother has died. There is no easy way to say this as she was shot in the Darling Harbor area early this morning." Kalum informed Kathryn Reiner.

The statement was followed by the deafening nature of silence. The Angela Bates look alike, sank further into her chair. The woman who displayed an assertive face at the door began to shake just a little and looked back at Kalum in what might be described as a mindless stare. A pause and then "What time?" she asked. Amy took up the story. "She was found around 5:30 this morning in Darling Harbour near the International Conference .Centre (ICC). As yet we do not have a probable time of death; early indications were that she had only been dead a short time, possibly less than ten minutes when she was found. Her wallet contained a driver's license. The likeness allowed us to make a preliminary identification though we will need to have her formally identified later. "

Silence is not always golden. Happily, short though in this instance as after no more than a minute, the double for Angela, began to talk. "She had led a simple and successful life. Enjoying good things but not overly opulent. Well at least while I and my sister were growing up. My mother was a woman who had faith, a protestant for many years, who in recent years become dissatisfied with her faith and her life.

"After my father died in the COVID 19 epidemic, my mother in her anguish began to distrust, God, me, my sister, and her profession. Apparently, she took small amounts from the business trust funds and repaid those amounts from future fees without anyone at first being disadvantaged. Then she snapped.

She missed my father. Suddenly she found life to be short and unfruitful. She wanted she said to live not just to survive. A saying she had found online. She developed a passion for having a better life, a more up market exciting life, where she mixed with those people who were excessively wealthy. Trips, shopping, and a new passion for high stakes gambling. She had, had enough of the careful life. She wanted some of the "glitz" before she left this life. I did not know she was stealing from her clients to pay for this new life till she was found out when she could not repay clients and then her arrest.

Getting caught seemed not to be of concern to her. She lived of her past experiences and dreams of what life might be. My father built a secure financial future but when his death robbed her of him my mother wanted to enjoy what she had and more quickly. For a while she made it, though on other people's money."

The tears were now starting to flow. Amy knew this was not going to help her solve the case, but it was what the daughter needed to get out, so she let her continue on.

"Though she lived here, she lived away from me and my family. Her grandchildren were treated with small things sometimes. She would rarely have dinner with our family, and she made demands of my husband to drive her to and from transport connections, so she only had to endure a short trip on public transport. She did not want to drive most days. To be free she said to enjoy"

"Did your husband take her anywhere early today or late last night?" Kalum chimed in at what he thought was pause in the eulogy.

"No not anytime yesterday. We were in bed together! I was awakened I glanced at the clock on the bedside table, and it showed it was just before 4:00 (0400). A car pulled up. Engine running, I didn't hear any conversation. The outside light came on so she must have left then. She was able to book a car service when she wanted, rather than a cab. She wanted to make an entrance."

"Could we see the flat?" Kalum thought he had picked another suitable time to pursue the case.

"Of course. This way. It is a studio rather than a Granny flat. My husband and I would use the flat when we are able to work from home. I am an ordinary everyday solicitor, and he is an architect. We could complete some of our work from here, as much as we can, so as not to be caught in in a long "chain" of traffic going into our offices or leaving work early. My oldest son used it as a place to live before he moved out of home. My daughter wants to live here once she starts Uni. I told her she would have to get Nanna out. However, that is now achieved"

In a moment they were there. The flat turned out to be another tastefully decorated area. A kitchenette, bathroom with matching washer and dryer in a corner one mounted atop the other. A small lounge area, television, data projector and a bedroom that doubled as an office. Clothes of Angela Bates were stored in a single cupboard, some jewellery in the bed side table along with miscellaneous papers that did not offer any explanation for the latest death by Cleaner.

Other usual office items included the twin laptop computers each with two screens mounted on a shared workstation in the bedroom. An iPad was visible along with another tablet, stacked so they could be readily identified on shelves in the work area without taking them down. Two printers one mounted on the other, along with various neatly stacked files stacked in low shelves against the walls in the work area. No phone for Angela Bates here or at the scene. A job for the later would be checking with her service provider on calls received.

xxxxxxxxxxxxxxxxxxxxxxxxxxxxxxxxxxxxxxxxxxxxxxxxxxxxxxxxxxxx xxxxxxxx

By the time Kalum and Amy had gotten back to the office, the on the ball Jennifer had by email passed on the contact information of the other immediate witnesses and her own details. What a woman thought Amy. She had (written, penned always sounds better) a short note to her less than patient boss; "The boss roared for a while, calling this the most sophisticated excuse he had ever heard and refused to believe it until a news feed to my phone showed me talking to both of you and then walking away from the scene. No pay rise but at least he sort of apologised and bought coffee for the office."

Amy showed Kalum the message and for the second time that day and for that week, both smiled.

32. Day 15 -The cleaner announces

An email went around to all the various hard copy and online news services.

Reference: "The Cleaner announces."

"By now you will have heard of my exploits", read the email that had landed with the media as well as the police, delivered by the ever-reliable Patrick Sliver.

Patrick had rung Amy and told her to expect it. It had been delivered to him by a courier service. The delivery fee was paid for in cash by the ever reappearing and disappearing Solomon left by the courier service in the "Silver" door mail slot. It was in a sealed envelope to be delivered to and only opened by Patrick Silver.

Instructions for Patrick were clear. Forward an email with the text as it was written, word for word to the police and as many media outlets as possible. Patrick even went as far to scan the envelope for prints, with him identifying those of staff member who received the envelope and telling Amy that there were other blurred prints, which would not be identifiable.

"How thoughtful of Patrick to scan the envelope," said Amy to herself knowing that Patrick was most likely right.

And so, the story from the Cleaner went:

Street Cleaner

"By now you will have heard of my exploits. I am on a journey at the end of which I hope to have righted the lack of justice imposed on some of our most serious law breakers. This is not a journey which, I sought to take. It is a journey I felt compelled to make. Given the apparent desire of our community for calm and peace and forgiveness over righteous judgement and punishment for perpetrators, the justice system so called, have allowed those who seek to disrupt our lives by their acts of selfish gratification the opportunity to remain at large and repeat their remorseless acts. People in a position to enjoy the money and the life style that comes with their position. But they fail to take seriously their responsibility for punishing a proven offender.

There is seemingly an acceptance by society of the light penalties handed out to offenders, law breakers. There is hypocrisy in the need to consider the upbringing of those who are charged and convicted. Even for those offenders who had the benefit of a secure physical and emotional up bringing there are always seemingly mitigating circumstances that are considered in sentencing. There is an overwhelming need to have everything in our justice system to be rehabilitative even when we are faced with perpetrators who can't or do not want to be rehabilitated. Justice is not done. Punishment is light or non-existent. I seek to redress these wrongs.

My journey will continue till we are rid of much of these vermin or till I am dead. I have no wish to subject myself to the justice system I so much scorn.

The elimination of the abominations of society, those men and women who seek to enslave society with fear, drugs, gambling, and other menaces to make people cave into to their wishes is my goal. It is my destiny. I am setting the example. I look for others to follow me. Not in some organised club with membership and annual meetings but for individuals who will stand alone with a single purpose of bringing real justice to those who have been wronged and real punishment to those who seek to enslave each and every one of us.

The media has decided that I should be called the Street Cleaner. Then so be it. I am the one who is cleaning the streets, taking out that group of people who need to be eliminated. Not reformed, not counselled, things that they who commit heinous crimes do not wish to use or be changed by, but who need to be eliminated.

There is more death to come and cleaner streets. Purity through Death. Removing the infectious rubbish from our community"

Amy and the team sat in silence, in a meeting room, on their first reading of their letter together. The silence as each person read their copy of the letter. Once completed each person continued to sit in silence. A silence with overtones of concern and anxiety, which flowed from each person's heightened sense of the need to stop what each believed, was a mad man.

Eventually conversation began on where they were with the case. Review of the goings on out at Coopernook. They discussed the delivery of today's message to Patrick Silver. Who was "Solomon"? A new summary of where they were up to was compiled to be distributed to all detectives, whether on the case or not. A loud rush of air followed a door being opened in haste and in anger as was evidenced by the door hitting the wall.

"Bible, you ok?" asked Amy as she looked up from the documents she was reading. Everything and everyone in the room had stopped, to examine the visitor to the room. The man often the one who tries to bring good cheer, looked as earnest, purposeful and inflamed as a……well he certainly was not his usual self?

Their thoughts now broken; Bible launched. "This is pure rubbish, totally vindictive. This man has established himself as the key witness, the judge, and the executioner. He must be stopped. I want to be there when you catch him. You will catch him. He may have been cunning till now, but he will make a mistake. His epistle today is a mistake. I want to be there when you get him. "

Then he left, slamming the door behind him with the same ferocity as he had used in its opening.

They sat for a moment. Bible was normally the supportive Sergeant who never really said a word out of place. A statement echoed by the Superintendent, who had said that Bible managed the squads and managed all manner of people whether the be the minister or new constable and everyone in between, in such a way that it freed up the Superintendent's time for "real policing", not being stuck behind a desk all day. This was a side of Bible the newer members of the team had never seen.

Amy explained to the group that Bible was largely a stationed based officer these days. "He was wounded in a shootout with a career criminal that did not want to be taken in. The superintendent was Bible's immediate senior officer when the shooting occurred. Bible had called in the sighting of the criminal and been told to wait for back up. However, the criminal was heading to a country airport and noticed he was being followed. He left the car. He and one of his associates decided to hide off the road and take out Bible who was following them. Bible was on his own as his partner had been seriously injured two days before and was hospitalised. The shots that were hitting the car as Bible approached forced him to try to drive the car off the road. He pulled up in a paddock after going through a wire fence. The crim and his associate continued to fire on the crashed car. Bible was bleeding but managed to stay focussed, left the car and returned fire managing to get across the road and around behind the shooters.

When our current superintendent and other back up arrived, the associate was down but still alive and the crim was dead. Bible was shot in the leg and the arm and had injuries from the crash. He was bleeding and close to passing out, which he did once placed in an ambulance.

Anyway, Bible was left with a slight limp he covers up by strapping his right leg in a brace. The limp is rarely noticeable. Though the upstairs group wanted him pensioned out, Bible didn't and the "Super" fought for him. He knew the qualities Bible possessed. You may not have noticed but the Superintendent always refers to Bible as "Bible" not by his rank or last name. They are both deeply appreciative and supportive of each other.

Street Cleaner

Bible knows his limitations in active policing. The superintendent has a respect and friendship with Bible which has lasted many years and will continue after they both retire from the force. I don't know that the 'Super' will allow his friend to be there at the end. But we shall see"

Part 6 – And then for a while there was nothing till...

33. Days 16 to 27-And then there was nothing, almost

No evidence of any activity by the Cleaner. Nearly twelve days had gone by since the latest message from the Cleaner while Amy and the team had nothing more to show for their efforts nothing more to show for their efforts.

Amy had been called to a meeting with the Superintendent. There was nothing new to report. Some small amount of pressure was now being applied from the office of the minister who was getting pressured by the state Premier.

A meeting with the team on Day 27 of the investigation brought up some new information on possible suspects. Johnathan and Aerial had been working with police commands and the courts around the state to collate information on men in the legal system that were outspoken about the lack of justice or more likely the absence of punishment in the justice system. Five names were now on a short list. Five is always a nice number thought Amy the rating of issue out of five was a long held approach to looking at options in management. Two a binary approach either his one or that one was too narrow. Five was the right number. Amy was disturbed in mid thought as Johnathan began the presentation

1. Sirach Andrija
2. Ramiz Doab
3. Charles Johnson
4. Raid Karama
5. Jules Patmore

"So, what do we know on each of them? We will have a look at what's in our report plus what else any of us knows. These are not ranked in any particular way. Happy to start anywhere on our list" Aerial responded to Johnathan's suggestion that maybe he could start with the only woman on the list

"Jules Patmore", started Johnathan. "She has been involved with a local group seeking tougher penalties for white collar crime. She apparently has appeared on regional television; she is in Wagga Wagga, (in South Western NSW) suggesting that Australia needs to strengthen its penalties for all forms of crime. 'Penalties are punishment not a basis for reform' she has used as a sort of slogan in pushing her ideas. She works in the local court system as a Chamber Magistrate. Patmore has been spoken to by her manager the public position of a group of which she is a member that are aligned to her position on harsher punishments, particularly for white collar crimes. Of late she has been less outspoken but still belongs to the 'White Collar Crime Justice group'.

Her immediate and extended family have no links to any extremist organisations. Her immediate family, husband who runs an agricultural business along with their children appear to be a country family that have done well in their jobs and through buying and renovating houses which have in recent years become a second business.. Patmore is completing a higher degree in law that would apparently allow her to lecture in law.

Not in the report is a comment from her manager that was not to be officially recorded at the manager's request. Her manager suggested that she is not the action type. Rather she is trying to appeal to the local population. He says she is more interested in being a federal election candidate upon the retirement of the local member." Johnathan concluded, "I would suggest as does the report that this woman is not the Cleaner. Though there is a fit in terms of profile, her location in a regional town and she being a woman would make her most unlikely to be the Cleaner."

Amy and Kalum along with Bible who had invited himself to join the group, an unusual but always welcome addition to the team, who provided an insight into cases not prejudiced by the day-to-day involvement with suspects all reviewed the report and quickly agreed on moving to the next possibility given the restraints that Johnathan had listed "Ramiz Doab". Aerial moved to the next possibility, "He was born overseas and immigrated to Sydney with his parents when he was a baby, less than one year old. He is the son of a Siri Lankan mother and an Indian father. The family lived in India before arriving in Australia. The father holds a Doctorate in agricultural development, food processing and related technologies. He has a part time position with a food processing and packaging business and also lecture's part time at two universities in NSW, The father also occasionally visits some interstate and overseas universities on short teaching tours. The mother has a MBA and works in finance.

The family are activists in that they support the local Indian and Sri Lankan populations in enhancing immigration opportunities for the two national groups into which each parent was born. They live in the Parramatta area which has a large Indian community.

The son has been more outspoken on the problems of immigrants coming to Australia than the parents. He has expressed his dissatisfaction with government policy on asylum seekers trying to enter Australia. He completed a double degree in law and politics. His position in the justice system is that of a Chamber Magistrate and as a supervisor of some non-legal staff at the Hornsby court north-west of the city.

His employment record contains a reference to him having been spoken to by a previous manger about ensuring his beliefs do not reflect on or affect his performance his job. His current manager does not see his beliefs as a problem and he the manager talked of the demonstrations that he attended in the nineteen sixties. They are a past situation which he believes do not affect his job performance.

The manager believes the same is true of Doab. The manager doe not just tolerate Doab and his ideas but encourages Doab to be involved in and speak out from a factual informed stance on current issues affecting people and their rights.

His current manager laughed at the possibility that Doab might be the Cleaner. "The Cleaner is helping us to clean our dockets" was the view of Doab's manager. He stated that he believed that Doab was of the same view. In fact, he believed that Doab had been following the case closely and had commented on the value of the work done by the Cleaner in bringing real punishment to the guilty. But Doab was not the Cleaner.

Doab has spoken at various rallies, and we have footage of him challenging drivers to run over him while blocking a road at one demonstration for refugee rights. He was picked up by police at that demonstration but released without charge.

He belongs to the same justice reform group as Patmore and has participated with local members of the group in demonstrations. Doab was also a member of the Army Reserves for some years but left four months ago claiming pressure of work stopped him continuing to be a member.

He served as a legal officer, mainly assisting in the establishment of supply arrangements with local suppliers, on a six-month tour to Afghanistan. He volunteered to go on the assignment. Doab accompanied an engineers' unit. Reserves are given opportunities to take on active service. Preparation for, if, or when they may be called upon to be involved in a substantial way in military action.

A possibility for being the Cleaner?" a rhetorical question sounded by Amy

Amy looked up towards the end of the summary when military service was mentioned. "Let's check on and get any available specifics of his military service. How does someone who might be seen as an agitator fit in with military discipline? Let's talk to the people at the top of this criminal justice group. What do they believe in? Actions planned? Any radical elements involved in the group? Support for other organisations etc. Surprisingly to her, Kalum volunteered to work with Aerial and Johnathan on collecting this information. Kalum was changing his spots so to speak as the case rolled on.

Amy as with many other people believed that a picture of person could be the entry to their sole. She looked at the picture of every suspect. Doab's face seemed familiar. As she looked at the picture thoughts of her brother Brett came to mind. "It is not Brett. But the look on the face is similar, young but hard, worn, and not the face of someone with a suburban view of life" she thought." Johnathan disturbed her thoughts.

"Our next candidate is no more." Everyone looked up as Johnathan spoke. 'Charles Johnson is a retired magistrate. He has been radical in his thoughts on justice and 'punishment forgone which he believes will correct the person that is lost'. This is his trademark phrase. We found out on the way here that he died of a cardiac arrest two days ago. His house is vacant. His sister, who is coming to Sydnee to organise the funeral was found yesterday interstate. She confirmed his death. No further consideration of his cleaning credentials required."

Five had become four. There was no longer a balance around a whole median number, in our list of possibilities. Maybe this list is too small thought several people at the table without expressing an opinion. On the other hand, the same people thought that even with numbers revised down it could be, not to large, not overly small, possibly just right. The list could no longer be five as Johnathan had reported. Charles Johnson was unwell for some time before died. Not an unexpected death. Thoughts again unspoken by some of the group went to the possibility that the Cleaner, though not Johnson, whoever it was, may be dead before the case(s) were solved.

"Sirach Andrija", Aerial tagged in. "Apparently his given name relates to a Book of Wisdom of Yeshua Bin Sira, written before Christ lived or should I say in keeping with current political correctness, BCE (Before Common Era)? His last name is not uncommon among people living in Croatia, his place of birth. His name is also the name of a well-loved hotel in that country. His first name equates to the English 'Andrew or Drew.' Smiles appeared around the table. Aerial was looking forward to a holiday in Croatia at year end if the case of the Cleaner had been wrapped up. Everyone knew of the holiday, which she had spoken of often in her excitement to travel overseas and wondered if the place of her holiday had produced the Cleaner.

Johnathan again spoke up, "Having come to Australia as a baby, he is involved in the court system as a graduate trainee. His supervisor nominated him as one who fits the profile we distributed around the state. Sirach is exceptionally bright, winning several scholarships to support him while at university. In terms of academic merit, he was runner up in his faculty for three years. In the fourth year he was dux.

He is not widely outspoken outside of work about his ideas. On several occasions, in the workplace, he has developed persuasive arguments in favour of punishment as a means of reform which have been passed onto other graduate trainees in the Federal court system where he works. Topics such as restorative justice where the offender can speak to and apologise to people, he/she has affected by their crime he has debunked with the aid of statistics as being in any way reformative of other offender or of value to the aggrieved. He believes in the reintroduction of sentences where a career criminal has their life terminated when their offences reach a certain point on a scale, he has developed regardless of whether they have committed a capital offence.

Andrija is apparently reasoned in his pronouncements. He does not appear to belong to any radical organisations, though his ability to argue for a particular point of view is supported by his acting ability which has scared some of his fellow employees. His supervisor has spoken to him about some of the arguments he has raised, and papers circulated to other employees. Andrija argues he is the devil's advocate in taking an alternative view from the popular to promote discussion. He claims to promote new thinking that he believes will lead to a review of how justice occurs in this country. He has been noted to appear frustrated from time to time when his arguments appeared to not be received well. His quiet demeanour and apparent persistence added to his physical presence, he is tall, lean, and muscular has apparently according to his supervisor made some people uncomfortable from time to time. However, in the opinion of his supervisor and of some other people that he works with they would be surprised if he was the Cleaner. A lot of talk was the consensus opinion of Andrija but not prone to action"

With no questions, Johnathan completed the list. "Riad Kuranda, whose parents though Australian has extended family in Morocco. Though raised here they also have returned to Morocco to work from time to time. Riad was borne here. His parents named him using traditional Moroccan names found in the area where his extended family lived.

Street Cleaner

He is working as a chamber magistrate, in a busy local court. Raid is well known in the local Moroccan community as being supportive of victims but harsh in his judgement of offenders. He has often been known to though not part of his job to give offenders a tongue lashing, which is centred on how lucky they were to get the light punishment they received. Several people have complained about his manner, but he has been defended by others as being right as he always advises offenders of the maximum sentence they might have received and how fortunate they were to get off lightly.

He has featured in local press as someone who looks out for the victim. He does not give interviews to the press, saying only when asked about his beliefs and actions that he is only doing his job. No radical links, though he meets with a group of legal people who have stated that they were interested in law reform. On occasion the group releases papers to the media on the lack of retributive sentencing. The offenders are not sufficiently punished to offset the wrong they do in the community. Riad has had sparse comments in the media and generally sticks to the line that his personal comments to offenders are all in the pursuit of justice.

That's it. You have comprehensive information in your files." Johnathan concluded

A slight pause, then Amy asked no-one in particular "Have any of them been to New Zealand in the last five years? Aerial and Jonathan replied in a synchronised response as if it has been rehearsed. "All of them."

"Alright let's contact local detectives and organise at least some part time surveillance of the three live possibilities. Not for Jules Patmore. I think we have enough evidence to tell us the Cleaner is a man even though in all other areas she may fit the profile. The various groups to which they belong, and for each possible suspect when and where they were in New Zealand" clearly addressing Johnathan and Aerial, and then to no one in particular she said, "I hope we have not cast our net too narrowly by sticking to NSW possibilities."

34. Day 28 -A suspect arrested

"We got him." The whole team looked and almost in unison asked "Who?"

"I think we have the Cleaner", announced the uniformed sergeant who stood in front of Amy, who was quickly surrounded by her team. "Where is he, who is he?" asked Kalum.

"His name is Gerald Sjögren, he was found hiding behind bins in a laneway in York Street. We identified him from his picture on his driving license. A patrolling officer spotted him ducking into a dead-end lane and called him out. Sjögren was armed with a weapon of the calibre used by the Cleaner. The gun and bullets have gone for testing. He had clothes which matched the description of the clothes worn by the Cleaner. The suspect was close to a private function where police were attending, a return to Society b Steven Nelle-Grass.

Amy's thoughts turned to the history of Nelle-Grass. No doubt he was in a restaurant close by for a birthday and jail release celebration. The media had proclaimed his release last week after serving his whole sentence. No desire for parole time. The return of the king he was a crime king. But she thought, which, 'police were in attendance?'

"Free when he walked from gaol. No one required doing any checking on Nelle-Grass. Amy had been in the arrest of Nelle-Grass who plead down to two charges from the original five serving three years instead of a possible fifteen. This Sjögren had been close to the party.

Thoughts broken as the uniform continued his obvious enjoyment in relating the saga. "When Sjögren was approached he shouted he was doing the work of the courts. The work he said that had not been done. The officer called upon him to surrender, which he refused. Back up was called and filled the lane. Outnumbered, Sjögren gave up without a fight."

The uniform seemed breathless and with her apparent ever-growing excitement paused. "Good work," said Kalum. "Is he in the cells here" A nod of yes, the uniform's reply. "Indeed, with a lawyer at hand arriving shortly", the uniform replied. "Okay, we will be along shortly. We will question him, in interview room 2, the bigger room. Thanks".

After the uniform took her leave, a seemingly concerned quiet overtook the room for a few moments. Great news, the Cleaner may have been caught. Disappointment that the profile they had built, and the witness reports gathered at much effort to the team members and to the witnesses may offer nothing in the resolution of the case.

"Well, maybe it is over?" stated Kalum. As much as police are pleased to close grizzly cases such as this one there was sometimes, but not often a tinge of regret for the work they had done that had not led to an arrest.

"Right Kalum in the interview room with me, Aerial see what you can find in relation to any arrests, misdemeanours etc. Johnathan check electoral rolls and civilian data bases. If between you, you do come up with local family, friends, any address or other useful locations then round up some uniforms and get out to them. No need to wait for us. Let's go Kalum." But as Amy and Kalum left the team room, Amy turned and called back to two in room, "you might take the new uniform who gave us the news as an extra support, to observe from a distance, guarding the cars, but not as a key person in the squad. She may find it all enlightening."

The interview room was at the other end of the building from the offices of their group. Greetings passed as they walked by various groups and single offices. Customarily they let a suspect alone for at least an hour. This was time for then interviewee to gather their thoughts and decide whether to confess if they were guilty or at least for the suspect to worry about their situation..

An officer guarding the door opened it for them with a courteous nod. Upon entering the room, another officer that was guarding the suspect, moved towards them and spoke, "I have been instructed to stay because of the nature of the crimes committed in case the suspect acts up."

"Ok," said Amy who demonstrated in the delivery of her response that she was not happy with the third officer in the room. She knew that a video was running in another room, and she had always thought that was enough but there were times when senior officers asked for, rather directed, a uniform to be in the room with the interviewing detectives. This was not the time to argue, even if she was sure she was right.

The suspect was around the right height. The clothing appeared to be the similar to that worn by the Cleaner. He did not look dissimilar to the descriptions of witnesses who almost always provided slightly different descriptions that differed in small ways. The small differences were usually taken as to indicate that the witness's descriptions were genuine. At the moment it was looking good, but Amy always held back here enthusiasm when a suspect had not been caught in the act. It could all go wrong, not the right person, a look alike, copycat. We shall see.

Sitting down, Kalum lead off, introducing himself, and Amy. "Is your name Gerald Sjögren?" No response. "We are here to ask you questions about murders that have been recently carried out in areas around Sydney. I understand you have been cautioned but I would like to remind you that this interview is being recorded and can be introduced into evidence should you need to respond to any charges laid against you." Still no response but the suspect's face was starting to redden.

"Ok we believe you may know about the murder of... Sjögren interrupted, "I am not a murderer. I am a patriot." The suspect rose from his chair. The guarding uniform police officer stood to his full height and began moving forward. The door opened with the outside guard being alerted by those watching the interview. Amy and Kalum were up with Kalum waving a soothing hand while moving around the table getting the man to resume his seat. He sat and everything went back to the way it was.

Amy and Kalum had the same thought. This could be a long day.

■■■

Street Cleaner

Aerial and Johnathan made a quick and successful search of Sjögren's life. He had a history of minor public place offences. There were some petty nuisance offences with no jail time.

Two cars were heading into the Eastern Suburbs, on the border of Randwick and Kensington. Maybe ten minutes if the traffic pulled over for the cars. They had sirens on. These would be cut within around 5 kilometres from the location. A group of eight officers were speeding to Sjögren's home address Johnathan and Aerial along with six uniformed officers. Five of them were designated for this job.

The other person was an enthusiastic young, uniformed officer who had been involved in the capture of the suspect. Her surprised supervising officer said that she, the uniform, had just come out of probation was keen and showed a lot of promise. He was assured that this was just training. The officer would be guarding the cars. A small smile broke out across the supervisor's face.

Sirens were now off and ii was all out of the cars. Four officers were at the front of the house, to act as guards and to turn away any spectators that came to the scene. Two officers went around the back of the house, there being no fence to prevent them from entering the back area of the property. One officer was guarding the cars.

Johnathan knocked on the front door to no answer. But around the back there was activity as the two officers approached a woman hanging out washing. "Excuse me madam" from one officer who had holstered his weapon. As she turned, the woman saw the officer with the weapon out and for some reason did not see the other officer without a weapon who was almost on top of her. "Excuse me madam is this where... "Half falling back with the appearance of fear in her eyes, she said, "Is this about Gerald?"

The officer steadied the shaking woman, "Would you be good enough to go inside and let my colleagues in who are at the front door? We will stay on you back deck."

After several moments the woman made her way to the house and went to the front door. Upon opening the door, Johnathan and Aerial who stood side by side on the front deck, saw the woman and could see straight through to the back door, with the house being one long hallway with rooms off to both sides. They could see both officers standing beyond the door without drawn weapons.

Hello, "Is this where Gerald Sjögren lives?"

35. Day 28-It was all wrong, a look alike, a pretender? No closer to the end?

"Hello, Is this where Gerald Sjögren lives?" The old woman nodded her head in agreement to the question. "Aerial introduced Johnathan and herself. "Can we come in and talk to you about Gerald? "

The screen door opened, and they moved to the first room on the right, revealing a well-kept but older person's lounge room. Doylies, on several small tables under vases of flowers, some flowers were fresh but others that lived for ever were plastic. A lounge and two chairs positioned to watch a television that was not new but certainly younger than most of the other furniture.

The old woman was trembling. Aerial was unsure how she should address the woman. Time passed and the woman seemed to be settled after spending some time adjusting cushions to her back and raising her legs which were scarred with enlarged veins, onto a small stool in front of her. "We have Gerald answering some questions for us. He was found hiding in a city laneway. Does Gerald live with you all the time? Johnathan said softly so a snot to alarm"

The old woman looked at Aerial and Johnathan with tears in her eyes. Not crying but the watery eyes of someone who seemed to be able to normally manage their emotions but was having trouble trying to manage with these intruders to her domain. There as quiet in the room. It seemed a long time had elapsed since they all had sat down but in reality, it was just a few seconds. It seemed longer given the tension in the room. Johnathan and Aerial waited and then she began.

"Gerald lives here with me. I am his mother. He found it difficult to move out of home, so he just stayed with me. He had a fiancée once, but she changed her mind and is now married to a prominent man in the city. Gerald took it hard, when she broke it off, but he already had problems.

He began having problems as he approached the end of high school. He started to feel he was not worthy of other people's liking of him. He had good friends, but he began to think he was not much of a person. He began to create and believe a fictional view of himself. As Gerald he was nothing, but he then started to believe he may be a character from history or a comic strip hero."

There was a slow intake of breath by the woman who began to sip water from a glass delivered by Johnathan from the nearby kitchen. He had noticed her laboured breathing as she spoke. "One minute he would be William the conqueror fighting Harold at Hastings in 1066. The next he may believe he was a superhero. These imaginings seemed to cheer him up. I saw most of his delusions. He for a long time was able to keep them under control at work. Repressed during the day but exploding out at night. Sometimes I became concerned by how far he took them and tried to convince him they were not true. However, at first the harmless things he pretended to be did make him feel better about himself. These delusions came to him most often when he was stressed, though they only broke out when he was in an environment, he found comfortable. Medication did not help. He tried to deepen his delusions to counter the medication.

He at first took on a job that he seemed to like. However, as he was given more work to do with tighter deadlines his delusions that I saw at home began to surface in the workplace. One unexpected benefit of having his job in quantitative mathematics was his meeting the young woman in his workplace who was his fiancée for a while.

She liked his delusional nature. She had put it down to play acting. He seemed exciting to her. But then he began to get delusions about her. First, she was being attacked by her parents. Then she was seeing someone else. Eventually it ended as his darker delusions dominated much of their time together.

The police intervened at her request when he began taking on a persona he adopted here, where he was threatening to wreck the house. His workplace also had a disturbance for which the police were called. He saw psychiatrists who agreed the delusions had developed into paranoia. Medication prescribed did not improve his situation, but he was able to repress the delusions better in the daytime. Storing the stress at work till he arrived home.

Eventually he left the job. He still works with numbers and is employed by an insurance company. They are happy for him to work at home for some of the week. Deadlines are not as tight, the job is not as stressful for him, but the paranoia continues with dark delusions playing out at home. Recently he has been following the news on this murderer the Cleaner. A friend said to him the vague descriptions seemed like him, but the same friend assured him that they were with him when two of the murders occurred. He was here when one of the others occurred and at work early on the day of the recent murder. He has developed a new delusion that he could also clean the streets of criminals who escape justice."

Johnathan and Aerial had almost as much information as they wanted. The rest of the conversation was about taking particulars on Gerald's movement on each of the days the murders had occurred. His room did not turn up anything new. His home computer was confiscated and would be checked by the technical people.

Aerial volunteered to ring Amy from the car. They left a poor aging woman, who told her story with a degree of calmness and with clarity who had now become tired. She was regaling one of the uniformed officers who was known to specialise in comforting those who needed to be treated tenderly. "Poor Gerald, the uniform was last heard to say as Aerial and Johnathan returned to their car

"Amy," said Aerial "we have ....."

****

While Aerial and Johnathan interviewed Gerald's mother, Amy and Kalum were making little progress with Gerald Sjögren. After the "I am not a murderer, I am a patriot", comment the suspect settled back down in his chair and resumed his silence. Questions about the various murders elicited nothing. The suspect raised his eyes and then his whole face in a grandiose glare and looked at the ceiling with the occasional smile which seemed to indicate pleasant thoughts or possibly a self-told joke, or a secret. It was only when Kalum who has been leading the questioning asked Gerald "Are you the Cleaner?" a question they had not agreed to ask that a response came.

"I am the one who cleans up those people who have not been punished. I shot and stabbed them all, so I and others could live in peace. I intend to rid the world of all that is bad. The evil government will brought down. The United Nations will be reformed. I want world peace and it starts here in Sydney. Peace and prosperity for all. I have the strength of ten men and the purity of 100 good people. I will go on and society will acknowledge me as a hero." He stopped, looked directly at Amy and Kalum, and raised his hands in triumph, which momentarily caught the two officers of guard and then went silent.

Silence filled the room for a few seconds. Kalum led off again. "Have you any injuries? Have you ever been to hospital?

:I stayed for a while to get better." "I don't want talk about anything other than my destiny" Gerald Sjögren responded

"Do you have your medication with you?" asked Kalum

 "I said I don't want to talk about anything other than what I have been born for."

Amy took up Kalum's line of questioning. "We have police at your house. Can they pick up your medication for you?"

Suddenly rage filled the face of the suspect. He began knocking loudly on the table but did not leave his chair. All officers watching were on alert. The door quietly opened momentarily, but the guarding officer inside waved his colleague away. Over two minutes, or so, the knocking rose and fell.

Quiet in the interview room again, when Gerald asked, "My mother, my mother, is she all right?" The tone of his voice showed apparent concern for his mother.

"She is fine. Just sitting talking", replied Kalum, "We are going to take a break. Can we bring back some coffee? We also have some horrible police biscuits, which you can dunk. Relax a moment we will be back in a few minutes." There was a sense of growing relief in the room as they left.

As they left the outside officer entered the room with another officer taking up his position.

Amy was full of admiration for Kalum in his grasp on the situation." The biscuits are surely not that bad. Though I have noticed you bring a muffin most days rather than eating them" Amy commented.

Amy retrieved her phone finding an urgent text to check her voice messages. The message was as they expected. Gerald Sjögren has a psychiatric illness. When she relayed the message to Kalum, his response was, "The search goes on. We will get him."

36. Day 32-Another dead woman-not quite

The arrest of Gerald Sjögren and his transfer to psychiatric facility had now become public news. The media were trying to ignore the presence of a police guard at his mother's property, was causing concern for not only Mrs Sjögren but for all the residents of the suburban street. But as with all the 24-hour news cycle, new activities obliterated Gerald Sjögren's transgressions quickly and the street returned to the anonymous, normal slow and often boring pace of most of suburbia Within two days. However, it did not take long for the Cleaner to act. This was the real Cleaner.

The woman of fifty-five, blond hair courtesy of chemistry of hair colouring, not more than fifty kilos wearing a floral dress, stopped outside the building in Chifley Square. Scanning the scene, she looked with blue green eyes through her prescription sunglasses to see if she could recognise the man who had called and said he had a job for her. A public place we could meet, close to his work he said.

As she started to walk with a latte in hand, she appeared to be just one of many shoppers in a mid-morning crowd, window shopping, entering stores, when in reality unknown to her she was waiting to meet a mass murderer in a coffee shop.

The woman did appear to be younger than her years. She could also have been mistaken for older. She could be easily taken to be around forty. Her appearance had been enhanced by the work outs she designed and delivered in gyms across the city. But there were some visible age lines on her face which appeared to be unexpected for a woman of 35. A few years ago, she had finished serving six months of an eighteen month sentence for defrauding the government out of more than one hundred and ninety thousand dollars over a ten year period. Certainly, among one of the single biggest welfare cheats, Australia had seen, but still not the biggest.

Belinda Pike, the name recorded in legal records was not her real name. Belinda had claimed government support during a long period of supposed unemployment, though she had been employed. She specially claimed money for a carer payment for her long dead mother. It all fell over when one of her clients, who worked for the Australian Department of Human Resources recognised her name from a file where a regular audit had been carried out to assess whether the circumstances for her claims still existed. A detailed audit of her claims and checking into her movements had been carried out with Belinda required to turn up to an interview. Belinda bought an unknown, unemployed actress who posed as her mother. The actress played the part beautifully. Belinda produced a variety of wage slips to justify her claims of occasional employment which earned little money. The wage slips, which accorded with tax department records. The government interviewer had a different story

Belinda's gym client reported to her supervisor that the Belinda Pike she had met was employed, and that she was providing paid exercise services to clients. An investigation was unable to find her supposed mother. The actress moved on quickly to other roles. Government investigators, observed her leading a slow but steady work life in providing fitness training and other services to individual clients as well to small group classes. Consequently, Belinda was identified as the same person as the person claiming carer payments. Arrested, charged with multiple offences of fraud, and making false statements, she was convicted but as part of a plea deal. Belinda repaid the money she had fraudulently obtained with interest and was given a light sentence.

What was never mentioned at the trial was what the other services she was providing to clients. Belinda claimed the only services provided were physical training and remedial massage both of which she was qualified to offer. Three clients were identified who all stated that the services were as Belinda had described. Something that the prosecution could not disprove. Belinda paid a taxation assessment and penalties based on cash declared as payment by each client, which left the bank account she had in her name with a balance of less than five thousand dollars down from $300,000.

The Department of Human Resources was happy with the cooperation of the offender. This was certainly not the case with other offenders. As the offender had cooperated fully and the money had been recovered with penalties, they suggested to the prosecution that there be no trial and that the penalty be light. A plea deal was struck and approved by the court with a short sentence. Hence Belinda was out of jail as soon as it was possible. The case fell away quickly from public view. No drama, all settled, no one hurt, nothing to see here.

The Cleaner happened by chance to meet the actress who had played her mother. Not that he knew that when they first met. He had met her at a club and asked the actress to dinner. A little alcohol and the actress became talkative. She spoke of secrets she had but would not tell. They have a high price. The Cleaner was amused and was willing to pay a high price, for secrets. They finished dinner and went back to her place. He more than hinted that he would like to buy a secret of two. She said you cannot afford to buy my secrets. He offered her five hundred dollars at which point the money had a sobering effect. "Two thousand" she responded, "for one secret, five thousand for three."

"Are the secrets that interesting?" "Yes" she replied if you are into crime" "A crime has been committed? Enquired the Cleaner. "Yes, in one case there has been a crime committed" she replied

"All right he replied I will step out and get the cash, another $1500 for one of your secrets if it is worthwhile." The actress could see this was not a silly game. She needed the money even if she just got the two thousand this would help her live till she started rehearsing for a play in a small theatre but where she had won a co-starring role.

Good to his word the cleaner returned with half an hour, with the money. "Here is the fifteen hundred. I want a secret relating to a crime. What is the secret?"

Gratefully accepted the out of work actress assumed her role and explained the case of Belinda Pike and got quickly to the punch line "and I played her mother."

The Cleaner had not heard of this case. He assumed that as it was concluded quietly, the media had shown little interest. "There are two more secrets about this person or some other people?" asked the Cleaner. "I have two more secrets about another person, but no crime has been committed. I would say they are more interesting than this one."

The remaining money changed hands. The Cleaner indicated that he was only interested in crimes committed. Arrangements were made for a future meeting including dinner. Words were spoken before the Cleaner departed. The key words from a possible future secret to be sold of unnamed person from the soon to be known and award winning actress were that in other situations not involving Belinda Pike, "I played her sister… the other time I played her widowed aunt. I don't know what other services she offered but her computer was left open one day and a page of shares was visible." Money maybe, exchanged next time. But the Cleaner had what he wanted. This was a new target. Belinda Pike. A new evader of justice to be avenged.

So now thought the Cleaner we will find Belinda Pike, apparently all but retired from work, who killed off her other identities before she did the sentencing deal.

Belinda paced slowly waiting with latte in hand, for the man who said he wanted to become a client.

The Cleaner turned a corner and Belinda came into his view.

Belinda saw the man and immediately regretted agreeing to meet him. She had heard the reports on the killings. The sketchy appearance of the perpetrator and of his choice of clientele for his killings came to mind as the man approached her. Was he wearing similar clothes of the Cleaner and had he placed a hat on his head in such a way to mask his eyes?

Street Cleaner

Still, they would be in a public place. Nothing had happened or could happen without it being noticed by the passing parade Belinda thought.

"Hello" he said, "You are Belinda Pike"? A question posed as a statement. "Let's grab a seat in a café in the Chifley."

The man started talking as he sat at the small café table, not removing his coat, gloves, or hat. "I want to improve my athleticism; I feel conscious of myself and don't like to be seen in public." A conversation began, discussing physical needs arrangement's to be made, costs discussed. Then a shift in the conversation as Belinda and the mystery man who called himself Geoff, not a name he would choose for himself, but it came to mind, moved onto other matters. "That sounds good Belinda. It is funny I seem to recall your name being in the news, certainly from somewhere or other. Not related to exercise but I can't quite place where."

Belinda looked up from recording notes of their conversation, a cold shiver moved through her body causing a slight tremor. Everything had been very businesslike till now. "I have been in this type of business for some years. The occasional article in the press and online."

"No it was something to do with the law." Belinda who had relaxed somewhat as the conversation continued now felt as she did on first meeting the man. Where was this going? "Nothing comes to mind", she replied trying to give an outward impression of calmness, while searching for a small aerosol pack of citric acid in her purse that though it would not have a lasting effect, would sting the eyes of an attacker, and slow him for a moment.

Street Cleaner

The Cleaner had, had enough of chatting with Belinda Pike. He had toyed for long enough. The café owner was in the back room. Though there were people passing their location outside the café from time to time it was now as quiet as it was likely to be. "You were convicted of defrauding the government. Served time but not long enough." The Cleaner looked up. His eyes now in view with enough of his face to show a facial expression that displayed hatred to his coffee companion.

The aerosol went off in the face of the Cleaner. The Cleaner prepared for a frontal attack, lunged towards Belinda across the table. His eyes were stinging. He was trying to pull out his weapon. She pushed his arm away, but he grabbed her again, with both falling on the café floor away from the table. She kicked out of his grasp, but he caught the back of her heel making her fall into a magazine stand near the door. Reading for café customers. Nothing was said by either combatant. It was all action. Belinda's fitness and self-protection training more than enough to match the attack of the Cleaner.

Now out the door, both wrestling, both with a level of skill. The Cleaner managed to subdue his opponent to the point where he could now draw his weapon.

"You are the first one with fight. But one of the last ones. It will all be over in a week. A watery grave for all. You won't be here to see the big show on the harbour" Belinda broke away. He fired at the struggling Belinda. She was hit in the arm and fell, but still rolled away as he fired again, the bullet ricocheting of the plaza floor and breaking a window.

Street Cleaner

He could not finish her as a screaming crowd of four women had gathered, with their screams attracting two men dressed as labourers, who turned out to be from a nearby work site in the area to buy lunch. They were running, shouting and then were on top of the Cleaner, trying to subdue him. The Cleaner had retained his weapon in the struggle. Seen by one of the women who had first screamed at Belinda's plight she yelled "watch the gun" The two men wrestled the Cleaner away from the fallen victim. Combined strength of the men was greater than that of the Cleaner. Though they were more able than the Cleaner he still managed to get his gun hand free and fire in the air. No match for a gun, the men released the Cleaner several metres away from the scene. The Cleaner sprung up as if the struggle had never happened and yelled at the gathering crowd. "You can die too." A speedy exit as the growing crowd gave way. At the same time sirens were heard.

Unknown to the Cleaner the police were now entering the complex. He actioned an escape plan devised in advance. The Cleaner was a street away inside a few minutes. A different looking man, now ragged and red faced to the person who a short time ago had been engulfed in two battles.

Belinda was still alive. Wounded, in pain and now exhausted. The two men who had challenged the Cleaner were spent and being treated for minor injuries from the fight by ambulance officers were now on the floor, backs to a shop window. Police were running with the crowd pointing and yelling at the emergency door the Cleaner had taken.

Amy and the team had now entered the shopping centre. All four with guns drawn. Kalum and Johnathan leading the group. Following quickly on the heels of the heavily armed uniform police, all of whom were now on the street. All were now looking for an unknown assailant that had discarded a coat, wig and had lost his glasses during his escape.

Amy and Aerial were only seconds in arrears of Kalum and Johnathan. "We should bag the clothing" yelled Amy to a fast-disappearing Aerial, who heard but was not stopping to bag anything.

On the street the police were fanning out into nearby locations. A tip had come in from a citizen, who hearing a news flash of a police action in the city and hearing sirens, happened upon a man, stripping what appeared to be 'flesh" from his face. The citizen after being threatened with a gun pointed by the man had rung 000. The message from the passer-by was processed and available to the police within three minutes of the call.

A cacophony of shouting, phones ringing, police messages from cars and their communication system all had the same message, "York Street bus-interchange inside the last five minutes."

Police cars came over the Anzac bridge from the west. The cross-city tunnel was being closed. Across the east police who had been on standby were being deployed from Potts Point across the city to Paddington. Traffic was being brought to a halt on all major arteries into the city. A Sydney landmark across the world the Harbour Bridge had been brought to a halt in both directions for cars and foot traffic. The Cleaner still on foot as he was heading southwest from his latest crime.

Street Cleaner

Several streets away from what he regarded as his crib in Harris Street, he was working his way through the streets towards his destination. As he passed through Darling Harbour he saw police on both sides of Cockle Bay. They had been joined by private security guards that had locked off the building they were guarding. Then a stroke of good fortune.

Though the message on securing members of the public where they were had got through to the International Convention Centre, one "sloppy" security guard had given up holding back the crowds exiting the centre after a matinee concert. Suddenly the crowd surged forward, with someone yelling about a crowd member giving birth. The security guard not wanting to secure anyone, said, "Okay let her through, you people in front come out the door and make room. Don't run off". He stood aside and most of the crowd surged. Some were not sure and stood for a moment, watching others leave. However, the temptation was too much. Hundreds mainly women made their escape, joining other people walking along outside. As the immediate crowd thinned, a cursory search by the guard for the pregnant woman came up empty. A story was forming in the mind of the security guard for his boss, and for the soon to arrive angry police. The Cleaner had joined in with the running, walking panicked crowd

The Cleaner now devoid of his disguise had walked across the open area in front of the centre and joined the whole crowd as other exits from Darling Harbour were closed off by police. Even so the Cleaner was moving towards Harris Street. Amongst a crowd hiding in plain sight, he moved closer to safety, up Ultimo Road onto and crossing the road, moving quickly though an education precinct to where he had a flat

Street Cleaner

with police watching the street but not seeing the Cleaner amongst other people who suddenly emerge onto the street. Police attention was diverted by the growing crowd now angry with having to walk in a different direction than most of them wanted to go. Angry loud complaints of having to walk further than they needed to.

Meanwhile, Amy and the team had left the chase, only a street away from the then location of the Cleaner. The city CCTV cameras had lost their target. If only this was London, thought Amy, a city which has the greatest concentration of security cameras in the world.

37. The chase was on, close but no prize.

Paramedics, worked on stemming the bleeding. A non-fatal wound but the bleeding was of immediate concern. No need to lose a patient to blood loss who did not have a life-threatening wound.

Not that Belinda Pike knew what was happening around her. After being shot and seeing the Cleaner leave, her mind switched itself off, knowing the body was wounded and needed to recover and she passed out. Now lying in a pool of blood, her brain still active, and her mind still alive but dead to thoughts at the moment. Being lifted. A bed. Where was she?

The police had been quick. They were in the building as the crime was ending. Most who were heavily armed were wearing what could have been Kevlar vests, had taken off after the felon.

The police that were left at the crime scene were not heavily armed. They carried the everyday police issue of arms. They taped off the scene and were getting statements from witnesses and viewing footage taken by several of the bystanders, who were quick to film the scene on their phones. The bystanders to a person said they had filmed the scene to help the police. Though some of the footage, if not most of it would be sent on to or more likely sold to different media organisations.

One of the labourers, who had separated Belinda from her attacker was giving an initial description, "And his hair looked like it was coming of his head." The descriptions were all similar but with subtle variations. He was tall. He was normal height. His skin was an off white. His skin was whiter than mine.

Overall, the descriptions were similar and supported by the photos and videos made. Though a fully accurate picture of the attacker who ahd disguised his real appearance had not been secured, there were plenty of side on shots at different angles, which could be used by a police artist to get an accurate, though not perfect picture of the Cleaner. The testimony of the victim Belinda Pike would also help, though it maybe a day or two before her help could be secured given, she was currently being lifted onto a stretcher eyes closed again oblivious to what was happening.

The ambulance was taking Belinda to the Royal Prince Alfred hospital, named in honour of one of England's Queen Victoria's children, the nearest hospital which had the necessary facilities available at this moment. The blood loss now stemmed; the short trip of eight minutes occurred without incident. All traffic had now stopped, which allowed the ambulance to travel along part of the light rail - tram system without the need for unnecessary speed.

Admission, examination, and treatment accomplished; Belinda was made as comfortable as was possible. She had awakened during the movement in the ambulance and was awake during the treatment, answering questions with clarity but once in bed, exhaustion overcame her and she went to sleep.

****

Street Cleaner

A few minutes beyond an hour had gone by since the shooting. The police artist had spent time piecing together a picture from the photos provided. However, he wanted the victim to review the drawing before it was released given as she was the only person who was able to see the killer's face. A reasonable proposal thought Amy though one which would cause a delay in the release of the picture. However, she copied the picture from the on duty police at the last location where the Cleaner was seen.

Amy and the team were now gathered around monitors viewing the known path the Cleaner had taken. He did not seem to get any assistance in his escape. Distant cameras placed someone who had his physique entering Harris Street and then an educational precinct. The camera was too far away to make out a definitive location but narrowed his location to a group of buildings in several streets. There was no visual of him going further

The city was open again other than parts of Darling Harbour and the western area of the city which included Ultimo, a large education precinct, where students were required to leave their location via Broadway, away from the secured area. The area had been cordoned off from Ultimo as far as the old fish markets and passed Wentworth Park, the scene of the city's dog racing track.

Police were continuing to arrive in the area in the biggest cordon that Sydney had seen both in the size of the area being secured, and the numbers of police on hand..

The team headed out to meet armed police in the area that had been identified, hopeful an arrest was imminent.

38. I am in trouble -Time to end it?

The Cleaner speculated on his decision as always with an audience of one, himself. "It was a poor decision. To try to take down someone in a crowded area in full day light. It was needed. Not part of the plan but part of the goal. Time to move."

The Cleaner packed quickly. He wiped down surfaces quickly with the bleach he had bought for this purpose. Doorknob, toilet, kitchen benches. Sweep up dust and dirt. Moving would not take long. Another unit, close by. Top floor. A view of the street.

Now around an hour or more from what he regarded as his failed mission. He left through a back entrance via a supply bay for a downstairs restaurant to the building next door. Using the restaurant's back door that was set off the road he entered the building where he had his new abode. No one was around.

Transfer without incident. No one seen. No one saw his movement.

Police were around the building but looking the other way when he put the mirror on a stick around the corner of the building he had vacated before entering the building next door.

Settling into the apartment he did not unpack. The apartment had an attic of sorts, where he stowed his gear. The attic had a false wall behind which he could hide unseen.

Parts of the wall could be slid back allowing for entry into a sound proofed area beyond. Bolts on the inside of his "cubby", secured his position. There were no apparent joins in the "cubby" wall. Once bolted in position the only way in was with brute force. A sledgehammer would do it. But if it reached that point it was a shoot-out with police or one shot to his temple.

He sat and wondered how long it would be before door-to-door searches began.

"I am in trouble -Time to end it. I knew it may come to this. Still if I survive to the end, I will take the crime Kings and Queens with me."

Through a small gap in the curtains, he could see the area, moving from left to right to change his view. A sight of people in the street below made him speak to himself, "I can see you, Amy.'

****

Amy and the team had reached the search area in a few minutes. Senior police discussed their door-to-door plan. There were a few buildings which needed to be searched. A heavy uniform presence was on hand. The uniforms moved.

Just as Amy and the rest of the team were about to begin their search, Aerial took a call. The rest of the team paused. "Hello, Aerial... Yes, so both are off work... for some time. Thanks. Both, Ramiz Doab and Raid Karama are not at work today. Doab has not been at work for several days." "Well we may be close to identifying him ", Amy responded as she lead her group off assigned uniforms to one of the houses which was not currently being searched.

The Cleaner felt somewhat relieved that the investigating team was not searching the house in which he currently hid. He could hear voices around the building but nothing to tell him where the designated uniform team was currently. He wondered what was happening at his old rental apartment, where a resident may have identified him from the police sketch possibly as someone who lived on the top floor.

He waited patiently in the hall for voices entering the building. Then the front door swung open. Searchers were here.

A message was being discussed. It was the discovery of the other apartment and that he had been seen running along a street of the general area of Glebe Point Bridge, which he knew, was not true.

Funny he thought I am here not there. A small smile across his face suddenly wiped when he heard the police talking a level below. At the same time as someone yelled on the ground floor. "Finish up in here. We are needed next door."

He opened the loft door in the ceiling in the apartment where he was now located. Through the door quickly such that the loft closed almost as quickly as it opened. He moved quickly but silently to the artificial wall in the loft, opened the concealed door and crawled in behind it.

"No one ...I'm coming down" came the voice of the person who was searching the apartment below.

Relief, distractions by the police of themselves meant he was safe at present. But it wasn't over. They could always search the building again.

■■■

The team gloved up and wearing coveralls were now involved in the search of the old apartment. "Nothing of any interest, apart from the notice board", summarised Johnathan as the forensic people continued their picture taking and microscopic search. "The right place but too late", voiced Kalum. They all stared at the notice board which was laid out showing the various victims in order of when they were killed. The latest failed attempt was seemingly squeezed into an existing pattern. Several known criminals were still to come and a big group at the end. Aerial took some pictures so they could follow up without disturbing any evidence.

"Well let's get to the hospital and see what the latest victim has to say. Stick together for the moment, till we get back to the… ". The phone in Amy's hand rang, with the identification of the caller on her screen resulting in her unfinished sentence. An unexpected call.

"Eli Korobiete, not someone who I expected to ring today". "Ah" said Eli, 'But always a pleasure to speak with you Amy. I have some news."
"Look we are busy at the moment." stated Amy trying to dismiss the call to return to the search

"But you will want to hear this." Amy waited silently as Eli went on.

Street Cleaner

"I have been asking around about your Cleaner. One of my contacts may have identified the man. My man is a mover of furniture and installs cupboards, you know the sort of thing. He was contacted by someone who wanted some work done. In the past he had a few scrapes with the law as did the person who wanted the work done. Both have not had any transgressions for more than ten years. They had met in prison and stayed in touch.

When he arrived at the premises to view and discuss the job there was another man there, who was finishing up a conversation with a woman. He knew the face of the other person but could not place it at first. He asked his customer who the woman was who lived in the building and who the man was that was leaving. The woman he was told is an actress. They both thought they had seen the man before. But as time goes on the memory fades.

Today I received a police artist impression of the Cleaner. Don't ask me how I got it. I circulated within my contacts. The two men discussed it, and several possibilities came to mind. One was your brother, which I dismissed quickly the other was a man they had encountered who was in the local court system. His name is Ramiz Doab. Though I thought the likeness was not as strong as they suggested. Though the shooter appeared to have make up on to disguise his face they had both looked at today's attempted attack on news footage and remembered the look he had when he was processing suspects. Neither wants any contact with police, but we are convinced it is Doab. Also, that it was Doab who had been visiting the actress. That's it." A brief silence followed while Amy collected her thoughts, not only had

Street Cleaner

Korobiete helped with the investigation, but it was also now clear that the team was on the right track

As Amy was about to respond, Eli Korobiete hung up without any closing comment. Amy thought for a moment. The rest of the team focussed on her while she considered what to say. There had been more than 100 possible identifications of the Cleaner. All had been dismissed. But for Eli Korobiete to call and make identification was more convincing than a member of the public.

Korobiete's face was one of those who was on the noticed board. Not too far in the future plans of the Cleaner. The pictures were arranged by date, exact dates for those on the list who had met their fate and by month for those to come. It was clear the Cleaner scoped one victim at a time within a given time period. The exact date for future victims.

"I think we have identified our Cleaner, it is Ramiz Doab"

39. "It will be over in a week"

Belinda was still sleeping. The doctor said no to requests to wake her. They failed to respond to Amy's requests, which become orders, which became beseeching and then shouting, regardless of who was asking. The doctor in charge as well as his colleagues who joined him in support as tempers rose and various doctors offered various sensible medical reasons as to why Belinda should not be awakened yet. Long term health risks, she is the victim and cannot be treated as a perpetrator. We need to give her time to rest. We understand the urgency but awakened too early and she may suffer from shock, which may lead to complications. All perfectly sensible

A uniform who had been one of the first on the scene at the Chifley Centre and had followed the ambulance to the hospital had taken notes of the broken conversations with the victim he had managed to have as she woke briefly when she was admitted. He had been selected for the task of guarding the hospital door. The first in should she be awake a university graduate with a memory steeped in mathematical theory, he had chosen to join the force, rather than be an actuary, a **quant** or to lecture. Third in his year, the top male given that women had now taken over as the dominant group in the faculty and filled the first two places of a group numbering more than two hundred. The average scores of the three first placed students differed by less than one third of mark. The next in line was five marks further back.

He had tried the corporate sector but the joy he had in mathematics was diminished in the application of his work solely towards securing financial success. In the few months he had been a police officer, he had been involved in assessing documents in accounting fraud as well as being rotated into street duty.

He spoke to a frustrated Amy and Kalum. "She said the perpetrator, told her she was the first one with any fight and something about being one of the last ones. He mentioned a watery grave. He told her she won't be here to see the big show on the harbour".

It was clear that there was more to come when the victim awakened. Amy would follow up later with the victim and trusted what the young officer had told her was authentic. She thanked Ethan Summers that being the young officer's name and asked him to wait around in case the victim awoke. Something he had been ordered to do anyway.

Back to the office where work was going on to identify the people from the picture on the notice board at the flats as well as from pictures taken at the latest crime scene.

More guarding of criminal lives required. Kalum would not be pleased based on his previous response. But they had to be warned of possible danger.

A plan for the next stage of operations to be developed given the information gained in the last two hours.

Part 7 – Planning and waiting

40. Day 38-Planning Day all round

The buildings were searched twice. Apart from the discovery of the Cleaner's initial apartment nothing was turned up. A few smudgy prints that, were not good enough for processing. They could have been anyone's prints. When seen the Cleaner had been wearing gloves. The rooms in his initial hiding place showed no presence of DNA. He was careful.

The scene had all but returned to normal with just a few police in the street in case the perpetrator returned and also to keep sightseers away from the building. The presence of police helped to reassure residents that the "threat" had passed.

The victim woke briefly and had confirmed the information that had been passed on from the initial interview and then she had passed out again When awake She said she kept having dreams of her almost death. The doctors had observed her and believed it was better that she was asleep than being forced to wake up and resume her life.

The crime scene had as yet not turned up anything useful. The gloves and hoodie found had stopped anything being collected in the street for the weekly garbage run that might be directly identified as belonging to the felon. Some samples were taken, and a forensic group had taken samples from the workplace of Ramiz Doab, which may be tainted given that his work area was used by other staff on his days off.

The team had knocked off yesterday around 7:00 PM (1900). It was another early start. Amy started the morning meeting with her team. "So, we know that there is something planned that is to do with water. A big send off. The question of where is not known. We could presume it will be at the harbour, though there are docking facilities at other places such as Darling Harbour, Garden Island and White Bay etc.

The group gave pause to consider the possible locations where the final unknown "event" on the Cleaner's calendar might occur. Bible was present and had joined the discussions from time to time as his other duties allowed.

Given most of central Sydney was ringed with sea. Several locations were discounted given the impact of the Cleaner's event would be minimal. It came down to two locations, Sydney Harbour and Darling Harbour. On a weekend Darling Harbour, built on and around disused tram sheds, was an entertainment area, with its restaurants and walking areas providing the foot traffic. However, as the Cleaner had removed a person from his list at Darling Harbour and most people referred to Sydney Harbour as the "Harbour", it was decided to concentrate their activity at Sydney Harbour with a contingency plan for Darling Harbour.

The question was when. It was to be on a weekend. Not likely this weekend. They did not know if the Cleaner had begun planning for this big event but given the failure of his last attempt to complete his list of felons who had escaped his definition of justice, surely more planning time was needed. However, no one could be sure that the Cleaner would not have his big show on the coming weekend.

Amy began a resources list. What would be needed? Manpower. General duties and specialised teams. She had

several people in mind she wanted on the job.
Communications, another person came to mind. Negotiators
in the case of a standoff.

Involvement of the water police. Vehicles, the bomb squad,
requisitioning of armaments. This was not going to be a lone
saviour or a small team. This was a major exercise.

Resources recorded. Locations for police. Plan B if it all went
wrong. The planning session was going to be the rest of the
day and into the next day.

****

From his new apartment the Cleaner who had moved out of
his area of concealment, could see that the street was clear
apart from a few uniforms standing around. No doubt
hoping, he would return to the scene of the search. It was
not going to happen, he thought as he had never left.

The Cleaner needed to ensure that he got the best of the
worse to his farewell event. Not a good turn of phrase. The
worst of rest of the crims was closer to the mark. Gather
together as many possible crims who would come to the
event so as to eliminate them in one final effort. An effort
that may cost him his life. Sydney Harbour was his chosen
location, now for the detail.

It was to be a harbour cruise with a substantial attraction.
This he thought was the best possible way to secure
everyone's attention. The cruise would became a make shift
prison. He had paid a deposit for a cruise ship for the three
weekends in the future. Today he would send off the balance
for his chosen date and finalised catering details, using the

name Mr. Plymouth. Personal invitations were on their way out by email to the organisations the intended victims used as fronts to legitimise their trade.

Once he paid for the cruise ship, he spent time writing and rewriting the general information to get the right tone. A business event but with a sumptuous dinner. The launch of new organisation who could supply their needs. Each invitation was tailored to the "industry area" in which the attendees were operating. Each invitee had been asked not to discuss their invitation with others. It was a matter of some secrecy as the sponsor for the night Plymouth Industries was using this event as a soft launch and did not want to leak any information to their opposition.

****

The business Plymouth Industries existed. It had been registered some time ago. It had an office in Southwestern Sydney which was almost always closed. One person had been employed to be in the office, with little to do but take names and addresses of people who wanted to attend the launch of the new business. The one person employed by Plymouth Industries wondered why they were needed. A sign on the window of the office proclaimed the launch of a new style of company meeting the needs of many different forms of business.

Two people had put their name down for the launch. A lot of reading and studying time for the sole company employee, a mature woman called Connie who was completing the final subjects of a degree. Occasionally her employer, Mr. Plymouth dropped by the office and had some work that needed to be done. But Connie had not seen Plymouth for several weeks. Occasional text message came in, asking for small tasks to be done, but even they had dried up.

The emails started to arrive. Connie looked at each one carefully. Each one had the date, time, and location of the launch event. This was followed with details of the event, contact details of the cruise company etc. Then the general wording for the invitation with instructions on how to customise the invitation to each invitee. This was followed by a list of invitees, information for customised invitations. Finally, an email, with instructions on how to follow up on invitations.

41. Day 39 Plans settled, but when will it happen?

The first weekend, saw Kalum and Aerial on watch from their vantage point over the Harbour, with five heavily armed male and female officers close by. There were heavily armed groups of specialist police waiting at a station close by on call. There were teams of police stationed at Sydney Harbour and Darling harbour out of the view of the public. More were on call as were a communication group and other specialist teams in stations further away.

Some reserve members of teams who lived within 10kms of the city could come from home. The nearest member of the lead team to the city had to be able to accommodate the rest of their team in their home for the duration of the operation. Any further away from the city and the team members were being accommodated at police headquarters or nearby at available stations. Suffice to say that more than 90% of the officers that were on duty at any one time were waiting in the city, inner city police stations or inner-city residences.

Over the several weekends the operation was running the space to accommodate people was tight in some locations with uniforms, detectives and specialist police units arriving and leaving in twelve-hour shifts. Some of the police chose not to go home. Sleeping on makeshift beds and in empty cells over the three days from Friday to Sunday. Some even stayed in the station beyond those days as there was a minimal number rostered on during the week in case of the unexpected. Everyone was instructed to be ready to go, wherever they were waiting.

Street Cleaner

Amy and Johnathan were at site B, Darling Harbour with another contingent of police at a close by station. The choice as to who of the specialist police selected would be at Site A or Site B, was decided by volunteers first and the toss of a coin to fill the last few positions. If nothing happened this weekend then the teams would swap for the following weekend until the operation was complete or cancelled. No one wanted it cancelled. The stake Amy and her team in this being a successful operation had had been taken up by almost all the other officers now involved.

The fact that the Cleaner was only killing the criminals did not go down well. Eventually he may get it wrong and attack an innocent or an innocent person may be in the line of fire at the wrong time. The argument he put forward was that only the bad were being punished had been pushed. Not a new approach, one put forward by the now deceased Mark "Chopper" Reid who lived up to his name but no one in the police was buying these arguments.

Operation Clean Up was underway. Weekend one had begun.

Conversation at both primary locations centred on families, discussion of what might happen after it was all over. Kalum and Aerial passed the time both watching and talking. Minds and eyes on the job but talking which kept them awake.

Kalum usually did not talk much about personal matters but responded to a question from Aerial. "I decided to join the force, while at university studying human behaviour. It gave me an insight into the need to moderate our learned behaviours as well as what we inherit from our parents. I changed my mind on the division of what we inherit and how much we are shaped by the environment in which we live. Originally, I subscribed to a 50:50 influence but changed my mind because of my study and our having our first child. I am now 80/20 in favour of what we inherit. We are very much a product of our parents. However, the twenty per cent which can be influenced by our environment is still a large component with which to work. I thought I should try to be a role model and make every effort to influence behaviours as well as assisting people to deal with what they inherited. Anything to do with social work did not interest me. I wanted to be in an occupation where I was out of an office working with people. The force also offered scope for advancement. I wanted a home and family like most people and need to earn an income to support myself and my family. Though the job is about catching law breakers, it has allowed me to speak with some of those offenders, some of whom have changed their lives. Some have not. They remain a product of their genes." Kalum concluded his response. A silence followed suddenly broken by Kalum resuming "and the job is what I thought it would be and though I want to leave the team to get closer to home, I will miss it. "

Amy and Johnathan also spent their time in conversation, talking but also watching. 'It's after 21:00 (9:00 PM), nothing happening. It is unlikely to be tonight." Good practice for next week" said Amy her face stretched into a broad smile. "I think should get together for breakfast with Kalum and Aerial at daybreak to see if there is anything we have learned from tonight assuming nothing happens." Johnathan responded with a slow nod and a "Yes", though his face indicated he may have wanted to do or be somewhere else.

"I will be buying". Johnathan replied "Sounds good" though his facial expression unseen by Amy only showed a slim margin of increased happiness. "So a fast food take away?" Amy smiling looked up a Johnathan. "I think we can do better than that."

Aerial had asked Kalum the question on the why he joined the force. Now answered she felt she should share her reasons for joining the police. "I joined straight from school. My parents told me I should be studying at university. 'You have the grades to study dentistry or pharmacy; you could help people that way.' I did not want to leap into a degree, which I was not sure was of interest to me. I had heard policing was secure and that people left with skills they could use in other jobs. I have started a degree in psychology and am slowly progressing to completion. At two to three subjects a year I have around three to four years to go to completion. I am still not sure policing is for me, though I am happy with the opportunities given so far and the training I have undertaken."

"Your doubts?" asked Kalum?" "The future" responded Aerial. "I want to finish my degree, but I am unsure whether I will practice. Should I further my knowledge of the force or get out and try a different career in several years' time?"

"Maybe you could be like some of those fictional detectives, some days a police officer and some days a psychologist, always switching from one role to another." He laughed with Aerial joining in. Laughter to make the waiting more bearable. A night where nothing happened.

42. Still day 39 Cleaner plans to recheck

Ramiz Doab checked his plans. No appearance scheduled tonight.

The staff employed for the cruise would be paid at double normal rates for the night. A carefully selected group, some of whom had been on the other side of the law at one-time understood that they were employed for a company launch the date of which was being fixed. Their employment covered one Saturday, day and night. They would be paid for the night whether they did anything or not.

He thought he had covered everything. Invitations to his harbour cruise yielded around a fifty percent return with around forty percent of the people invited accepting, while the other ten percent declined. Some of those that declined asked that they be invited to future events. No chance of that.

Ramiz was happy that with a week to go, everything was proceeding well. He checked on the cruise company. He checked on the catering. The cruise was set for 8:00 PM on the following Saturday. The cruise was set to go.

There was nothing more to do or to say for his evening.

Part 8 – It ends – badly – how else?

43. Day 43 Nothing has happened-A little down time.

Amy waited just inside the door of the restaurant. She had another dinner date with her admirer. They had picnicked together went to an art gallery and ate take away at her place while watching a movie from one of the streaming services. She was feeling some affection for this man or maybe a little more.

The case still occupied her mind, but she was determined to enjoy the night. A nice restaurant a nice meal and interesting conversation it was set for a perfect evening. He had arrived and holding hands they made way to their table. Entrees came quickly with the conversation flowing naturally.

The conversation had become more searching over the last few dates. Amy thought "Mainly I am searching for what I like and want out of life", with he responding to a question from Amy. He asked about how she felt about children as a follow on to a story of his niece having hidden so well in a game of hide and seek, he could not find her. Amy thought I have not thought about having children. Let alone being married. I have always been involved in the job. I have been learning, developing, and experiencing new things in the job.

However, Amy gave the customary answer, "children would be great one day. Possibly one of each through it sounds like I am picking a car or a house." More laughter and he replied by saying he would like to have children and one of each would suit him fine.

Street Cleaner

The conversation over time had touched on preferred places to live, lifestyles, houses or units, preferred cars etc. Amy till now had been a person who liked to be in the moment. No life plan, just taking on every opportunity as it came along. Though she had been out with several men over before, without forming any permanent attachment this time it felt different, very much about deciding whether there was a life together.

How would my life change? Would I be able to follow a path of my choosing? Would I be expected to stay at home with the children? Children she thought, I know I said one of each would be nice but in reality I am not sure I want children.

The evening continued. A quartet played romantic music. Another lovely evening finished with a pleasant trip to her flat. Yes, she thought I am falling for him. There is more than affection. I wonder, I hope he feels the same.

44. Day 46 "An explosive outcome"

Jonathan, without apparent reason raised the subject of Brett while waiting to see if the Cleaner was to be around on this Saturday evening. Did the presence of Amy spark a thought in Johnathan's mind?

"I usually hear from Brett every few weeks, but nothing for nearly a month. I know Brett likes to know what is happening. He is natural snoop that must help him as a private detective." responded Amy

"He does belong to one of those groups who talk about the inability of the law to bring about permanent solutions to repeat offenders. The group believes the smartest felons rarely get caught and those that do seem to carry on their activities from inside prison. One day he started detailing the workings of modern-day star chamber."

Amy stopped talking. The visitors to the Harbour Cruise were now arriving, some quietly and some with considerable noise. Amy spotted a small-time forger who had some years back had been attempting to print his own version of fifty-dollar notes. Other criminals known to Amy joined a crowd of happy voyagers' boarding the boat. Everyone loves a catered Harbour Cruise. When Eli Korobete arrived a few moments later, Johnathan was dialling Kalum's number as he said to Amy. " This looks like it." Kalum was at the alternative location in Darling Harbour with Aerial.

"Kalum, we have observed a number of criminals boarding a ferry here at Sydney Harbour. I suggest you redeploy everyone to this location. Kalum had no questions uttering just the words "Will do", while signalling to Aerial who was walking the hall adjacent to the room. They began contacting people on each of their lists which they had split between them earlier. Within five minutes sf contact with Johnathan, Kalum and Aerial were running to their car. The special crews had started to leave their current location and were making their way to Sydney Harbour. Commanders of these crews were contacting commanders in the reserve units to take up a position at Darling Harbour. This was a large manpower operation.

****

On the boat the Cleaner was pleased at the number of people boarding the ship. Everything was in place, and everyone was in place.

Explosives had been attached to the boat below the water line concealed in a hollowed out propeller. Police divers had surveyed all ships/boats in the Harbour to check for explosives. Divers worked below and dogs above on the boat. The false propeller had been fitted at night by a small number of divers who attached it as an additional propeller. Suitable tags were painted on the blades indicating it was an experimental propeller being used to reduce friction between the boat and the water. There had been talk of this new experimental propeller in the media over some weeks. Most of the talk emanated from the Cleaner who had his office staff of one send out a variety of press releases citing research conducted overseas. Though it really did not matter as the Cleaner had ensured that the propeller was fitted a day after the water police inspection. He had gained access to the inspection schedule.

Street Cleaner

It was a few minutes to departure when he saw Eli Korobete and several of his associates board the boat. An associate soon after boarding was on the phone. The Cleaner noticed the associate pushing past other attendees to get to Korobete. At the same time the ropes for the moorings were being pulled up and put away as the engine began to propel the boat away from the wharf. Korobete was in a deep conversation. His phone rang. He looked up and around and spotted the person he now knew was the Cleaner.

****

On the other end of the phone was Amy who was telling Korobete that the Cleaner was on board, and he should get off the boat and take as a many people as possible with him. Though he doubted her at first, he looked up and around and spotted the man he now was sure was the Cleaner. A moment of thought and then he said as she terminated the call "I am about to leave"

The Cleaner was looking straight at Korobete as Korobete looked at him. He also noticed that there was action on the wharves with heavily armed police running towards the boat yelling for the captain to stop. The Cleaner went onto the bridge of the Boat, pointed his gun at the captain and ordered him to continue on. At the same time the Cleaner pulled a different phone from a cupboard on the bridge.

Korobete yelled loudly to anyone who could hear him over the raucous conversations occurring "get off the boat this is the Cleaner's Boat." He and his associates were the first people to jump into the water. As he came up and prepared to swim, he yelled again "get off the boat" and started swimming Some of the passengers paused on hearing Korobiete's while others most of the crew and hospitality staff decided to jump.

****

The Cleaner with the newly obtained phone in his hand entered a number pressed the call button and the sky was alight as if it was the world famous New Year's Eve fireworks on Sydney Harbour. Only this was not crackers it was deadly explosive. People were jumping off the boat. Some were propelled into the water more quickly than they expected. Some did not move.

Bodies ripped apart would be unrecognisable. Water Police with tankers who were on stand-by had raced into the scene as the explosives went off. Water began to be sprayed onto the boat. One hose was directed at people falling into the water who were on fire.

Windows had been broken on both sides of harbour. The building known as the toaster on the Botanical Gardens side of the docks seemed to have every widow broken. The Museum of Contemporary Art on the opposite side of the harbour had windows broken and some of the outdoor furniture in the grounds broken from their base and blown into the air. Some people, ordinary civilians were on the ground injured. Young lovers just passing by the scene were now casualties. The boat was burning with still some people who were on the deck and on fire jumping off the boat. Amy wondered how anyone could have lived through that blast.

Street Cleaner

Police on the dock rushed forward. And there were ropes extended out to pull people from the harbour. Ambulances were on the scene with paramedics giving attention to the people who were brought up onto the wharves from the water. Different group commanders were telling their teams to spread out along the wharf and get people to the paramedics as soon as possible. Amy and Bible were trying to board the vessel. Bible had joined them. No one questioned his presence.

Johnathan and Kalum were in the water trying to move the injured as well as lifeless bodies as close as possible to police officers who had dropped ropes into the water. Aerial was working on one of the rope lines with another officer. She had in less than ten minutes already helped three people escape the harbour and begin treatment with the increasingly busy paramedics.

Shots rang out. Some of the people in the water were currently wanted. They tried to get away from the Police. When they felt the police were too close, they fired in the air or directly at the police officers.

There was a pause for a moment. Then the police brought from Darling Harbour stepped forward and fired back but high over their heads. The weight of gun fire by the police was enough to cause the felons who had fired first to surrender. Several people pulled from the water where the shots were fired on the police had bullet wounds. The rescues and the arrests of everyone pulled of the boat and out of the water continued unabated

Street Cleaner

Amy and Bible now on the ferry deck eventually started to see the boat or what was left of it emerge form under a spray of water. Steam mixed with smoke was starting to emerge. They nodded to each other and climbed of debris on the still burning boat which had now slowly crashed into a wharf. Amy went left and Bible went right. Both had their guns dawn not taking any chances. Some people were lying on the deck moaning. They both encountered people that had been badly disfigured by the fire.

Bible burst through a cloud of smoke and happened on the Cleaner. The Cleaner saw Bible and the gun he was carrying. In an act of desperation, the Cleaner raised his gun to fire. Bible fired three times. Each bullet hit the man. All three were fired into the upper body. One of the shots was fatal, a shot to the head.

Amy came across the boat in the direction of the shots. Bible was standing looking at the body of the man that had ruled the streets through threat and death in the last two months. Now dead. Bible turned to Amy and said "vengeance is mine says the Lord."

45. It over – just the mop up to go

A week had passed from that dreadful night and the Superintendent was sitting in his office with Amy sitting opposite.

"The initial count" stated the superintendent, "of the ninety-seven people who were on the boat forty-three are dead. Thirty-six were invitees. The others were crew members or part of the hospitality employees. As a result of the deaths, it appears we have made arrests so as to have cleared eighteen different cases.

Of the remaining fifty-four, six are likely to die. However, we have arrested thirty one fugitives who are alleged to be involved in twenty seven cases. Two cars of people who arrived after the ferry left the dock have been held and stand accused in five cases. The total number of charges made against those people still alive is three hundred and ninety-seven.

I have spoken with the Commissioner. He is not happy with the number of innocents who have died but he in turn has spoken to the minister who is more than happy with the number of charges laid and cases cleared. You and your team will receive both applause and some criticism from the minister. However, the divers that cleared the boat of explosives and the water police who investigated the hiring of the ferry are in for a pounding.

There will be an investigation into the finalisation of the case, but I am almost certain that those above want to reward you, your team and dozens of others for their efforts on the night. Bible is amongst those who will be honoured. I should add that everyone is happy that the Cleaner is dead. Who fired the fatal gunshot/shots is a bit of a mystery. I understand you will be confirmed as a Detective Inspector. Kalum as a Sargent along with Johnathan while Aerial will go to senior Constable and will be asked to sit the sergeant's exam"

The Super knew very well that it was his long-time friend Bible, who had turned up to work after just two days off to resume his normal duties. Bible behaved as if nothing had happened. "Just smoke I inhaled from a fire. It made me very tired." he said when he was asked about his short absence from duty. But news was spreading fast as to what really happened.

Amy was not interested in plaudits. She wanted herself and her team were to be cleared of any wrong doing. She knew that the Super knew it was Bible who killed the Cleaner. He was not going to let on that he knew.

Eli Korobete and several others of the invited guests extended their thanks for the warning. They knew that they had escaped the explosion because of Amy's actions. Some questions to answers but Amy was pleased that all round everyone seemed pleased that the reign of tyranny was over.

46. Day 50 -"Does it ever end?'

Bible exited the building just as Amy was kicking litter into a heap. Local young people dropped beer bottles, cigarettes butts and worse on the street near to the "office."

"Are you the new Cleaner?" with a significant emphasis on the word Cleaner' joked Bible

"Sure, lets you and I clean up clean up these streets and the stationary cupboard and filing room while we are at it," replied Amy

"Bible I have something to tell you, a secret...."

Johnathan and I – "a jack hammer digging out a piece of footpath that had needed replacing for more than a year interrupted Amy.

"I could not hear you' responded Bible.

"Johnathan and I are..." with the jack hammer breaking into the conversation again.

"I can't hear you," laughed Bible. "It does not matter I see Aerial coming."

"We may have a new case" Aerial said to both. "Remember, Anosmia Smith the disappearing non witness he has been found dead."

Street Cleaner

"Well, another new case" remarked Bible and then continued as they walked in "Amy what were you going to say?"

"It can wait dear sweet Bible we now have the case of the murder of Anosmia Smith to occupy our lives ".

On a corner not far from where Amy, Bible and Aerial had been standing a figure dressed in sweatpants and a hoodie concealing his face peaked around a corner trying to listen to their conversation. He turned and the letters SOL MON with a space probably for another O between L and M on the back of his track suit top walked quickly, without running and blended into the city crowds.

www.ingramcontent.com/pod-product-compliance
Lightning Source LLC
Chambersburg PA
CBHW072355110726
47909CB00003B/713